Handy One
A Reba Rose Parker Psychic Mystery

Book 1

Jenna B. Neece

Copyright (c) 2019 Neece Editorial Services & Publications

All rights reserved. Copyright under Berne Copyright Convention, Universal Copyright Convention, and Pan-American Copyright Convention. No part of this book may be reproduced, stored in a retrieval system, or transmitted in any form, or by any means, electronic, mechanical, photocopying, recording or otherwise, without prior permission of the author.
ISBN:
Library of Congress Control Number:
Any reference to historical events, real people, or real places are used fictitiously. Names, characters, and places are products of the author's imagination.

Front Cover Design: Jenna Neece
Second Printed Edition, 2019.

Neece Editorial Services & Publications
Stillwater, Oklahoma.

Copyright (c) 2019 Neece Editorial Services & Publications
All Rights Reserved

Dedication

To my mother. Thank you for always believing in me.

HANDY ONE	1
Dedication	4
Chapter 1	8
Chapter 2	20
Chapter 3	26
Chapter 4	32
Chapter 5	39
Chapter 6	47
Chapter 7	53
Chapter 8	61
Chapter 9	68
Chapter 10	76
Chapter 11	83
Chapter 12	92
Chapter 13	101
Chapter 14	107
Chapter 15	115
Chapter 16	121
Chapter 17	127
Chapter 18	134

Chapter 19	143
Chapter 20	151
Chapter 21	156
Chapter 22	163
Chapter 23	169
Chapter 24	177
Chapter 25	183
Chapter 26	190
Chapter 27	196
Chapter 28	204
Chapter 29	210
Chapter 30	216
Chapter 31	222
Chapter 32	228
Chapter 33	234
Chapter 34	240
Chapter 35	246
Chapter 36	252
Chapter 37	263
Chapter 38	272

Chapter 39

Chapter 1

Sometimes a walk in the park can actually change your life. That's exactly what happened to me the day I decided to snap some photos at the local hiking trail in the quaint little college town I live in. Everything seemed ordinary until I got home and started looking through my shots of Stillwater's mid-morning beauty.

Now, it's important that you know a little bit about Stillwater. It's located in the middle of Oklahoma. Stillwater straddles the boundaries of being more than a town, but less than a big city with its population of about 50,000 people. Our population changes a lot throughout the year because of the large student population. Most people consider Stillwater to be a quiet enough little town without that high of crime rate, which is why I never expected what happened the morning I was snapping photos of some of Oklahoma's prettiest nature.

As I scanned through the images on my camera, I noticed something in the corner of one of my shots I snapped near the lake. I zoomed way in to see what it was, and that's when I realized it was a hand.

I'm not talking a doll hand or something. I'm talking a freaking human hand. I know what you're thinking, how could I be sure it was real? It might have something to do with the red drippy stuff on the end. Dolls don't bleed last time I checked.

I sat there just staring at it a while before I decided I'd better go back to check it out. I know, I know, I should have just called the police. But what's life without a little adventure? Calling the cops for no reason isn't a joke these days. Figured I should make sure before I raised a fuss.
I crated my little spunky red dachshund Ozzie, and I went out and hopped in my trusty Honda. I guess I wasn't

thinking much about what I'd do when I got there until I pulled up in the lot and found six police cars there.

Uh-oh. This didn't look good. You see, this put me in quite the pickle. Did I get out and tell them what I'd seen or turn around a leave as fast as I could? Well before I could make up my mind, a fine on the eyes, clearly cocky cop approached my car. I rolled down the window.

"Can I get your name Miss?" the officer said.

"Reba Rose."

"Well, Miss Rose…"

"Rose is my middle name."

"You have a last name, right?"

"Parker," I said with frustration.

"Well, Miss Parker, why are you loitering at a crime scene?"

By now I was getting plum pissed off. I wasn't loitering. I was coming back to investigate and see if there was a crime!

"Well, I'm actually coming back for the second time today. You see, I'm a photographer. Earlier I took some shots out here, and when I got home, I noticed something weird in one of them. I came back to check it out."

This clearly piqued the officer's interest. "What exactly did you see?"

"Well, it looked a lot like a bloody hand."

"You're telling me that instead of calling the police, you decided to come back and check out a possible decapitated and bloody hand on your own?" said officer smart-ass.

"Well, I don't believe in wasting the efforts of the police. I figured it couldn't hurt to come look before I swung by the station."

The look of disbelief that officer asshole was giving me was enough to curl my hair. Well, actually, the unusually hot and humid April day was frizzing out my curly reddish-brown hair like a steamed up bathroom, but that's not the point.

He said, "Ma'am, I'm going to need see those photos, but in the future, I want you to leave matters to the police. You could have contaminated the crime scene."

"Good God, I wasn't going to touch it. I was just gonna take a peek!" I spat out in irritation.

Officer Asshole rolled his eyes at me and replied, "Hair, footprints, anything can contaminate the scene. This isn't tv. We have to be careful."

I swear to God his eyes lingered on my frizzy bush covering my head. A drop or two of sweat rolled down my brow as I reached for my camera in the seat beside me. I scrolled through the photos until I found the one in question. I zoomed it way in and handed the camera through my open car window.

Then I asked, "You have a name, Sir?"

He looked up distracted and said, "What time was this photo taken?"

I took the camera back and checked the time stamp. "About 10:45 AM," I said.

"Are you sure?"

"Yes," I said, "look here." I handed him the camera with the stamp displayed. He frowned.

"Sir, what's wrong?"

"Stormy."

"What?" I said as I looked up at the bright blue sky.

"Officer Calvin Stormy is the name. I'm going to need you and your camera to come in for some questioning at the station."

I stared back at him like he was a wolf in a sheep pack. What the hell had I gotten myself into? I didn't do anything. Why should I have to come in? He turned to walk away from my car with my camera in his hand.

I hollered, "Where the hell are you taking my camera? It cost a fortune!"

He looked back at me with humor, and said, "It's evidence now, Ma'am."

I swung the door open faster than a cat exiting a car engine. He was NOT taking my camera. I was spitting mad, and as I marched after him, I passed under a campsite light. It shattered.

Well shit. Six guns drew at the same time, and Officer Stormy hit the ground. They thought I'd shot at him, but truth be told, I burst the glass bulb with my energy.

You see, I have abilities. I don't like to call them psychic powers because it makes me think of those late at night commercials where the person holds on to the crystal ball while humming. Yeah, I just like to call them my abilities. I don't want to get locked up in the loony bin for the wrong person figuring out about them. Now I was stuck standing there with a metaphorical egg smeared on my face and weapons pointed at me. I clearly should have stayed in bed today.

I said, "Whoa, whoa, guys! You think I broke the light? Please lower your weapons."

They all looked so shook and embarrassed you'd think they could see the ghost I'd just noticed looming a little ways away. Of course, they couldn't though. Officer Stormy said, "Lower your weapons. Clearly, it was a freak accident. She's not even holding anything." They all lowered their guns and hastily turned back to what they were doing.

He walked back towards me, and much to my dismay, he said, "How in the bloody hell did you do that?"

"Do what?" I asked innocently.

"Somehow you just exploded that light. I'm not a moron. It's daytime. There isn't any power to it. There is no way that it just blew up."

"And how do you think I managed to spontaneously burst that light? It's not like I'm a witch," I said as sweet as my angry ass could manage.

He was perplexed, but pressed on, "No, of course, you aren't a witch. Those aren't real. I don't know, but my gut tells me that you could blow that light up again if you so desired. Look, I'm not taking your camera forever. I just need to take it down to the station where we can back it up. Then you can have it back. I will need you to answer some questions for me as well."

"Fine," I said with irritation. "I need to get home, so can we go right now?"

"Why such a hurry?" He asked. "Going somewhere important?"

"No, well sort of. I need to feed and walk my dog. Let's go."

As I turned to walk back to my car, I realized I'd been just a little too slow. The ghost of a man, who appeared to be about mid-fifties, was leaned against my car door.

Now let me tell you, I hate ghosts. They never know that they're dead at first. They always get emotional when they find it out, and good God, I hate having to walk through them. It makes you feel all cold and icky. They just make my skin crawl.

The ghost looked at me hard and said, "Lady, why won't those damn cops talk to me, but they all gave you their full attention?"

I pondered my options. I couldn't answer out loud, and I hated to open the door through the guy, but Officer Stormy was still watching me. I could hear what he was thinking loud and clear. He wanted to know more about me, how I'd blown up that light, and what my ass looked like in the thong I was wearing. My thong had clearly peeked out of the top of my yoga pants. Typical man. Always thinking about ass in one way or another.

I yanked the car door open and plunged through ghost guy. He might have died with fright if he wasn't already dead. He said, "What the..."

I slammed the car door and turned my head at an angle where none of the cops could see. "I'm sorry, but it appears you're dead."

I put the car right into reverse and backed out before he could say another word. The last thing I was going to do is let Stormy see me shaking. I wanted to get the hell out of dodge before anything else happened that might get me a one-way ticket to the psych ward.

Now look, I know there are more important things at stake than if people thought I was a crazy, but to be fair, there is nothing quite like the look people give you when they know that there is something different about you. It always takes me back to the way people just flew out of my life once they realized I had health problems, sometimes was almost debilitated due to my health, and wouldn't likely ever have a cure for my mystery ailments.

People don't think disability is pretty. They think it's gross. They think it's painful to look at, and most people think that disabilities that are not visible might be fake. I pondered all of this as I drove away back to the town center where the police station is located.

Chapter 2

Two hours later, I was still in a crappy little holding room waiting to talk to the chief of police. Apparently, he had quite the list of questions for me. He probably thought I was totally nuts, but as long as I was as truthful as possible, I figured there was no way I could get into any trouble. I'd done nothing wrong. I'd simply been in the wrong place at the wrong time. At least that's not a crime.

An older, graying man walked in the room in front of Officer Stormy. The older man extended his hand and said, "I'm Police Chief Neilson. Please call me Shawn."

I reached to shake his hand, but when my skin touched his, I visibly shuddered.

There was blood everywhere. Dripping from the dark mahogany table onto the floor, splattered on the cream colored curtains, and seeping from the gaping wound on the dead man's neck. He laid there face down on the floor. Soft glowing light filled the window as sirens blared in the distance, but they didn't seem to be getting any closer.

I yanked my hand back. It felt as if the room had been drained of all air. I felt the color seep from my face. The room spun viciously around me.

Officer Stormy and Chief Neilson looked surprised. I must have gasped out loud because the chief said, "Ma'am, are you all right?"

I opened and closed my mouth a few times before I mustered up a, "Yes, just feeling a bit unwell."

"Understandably," Chief Neilson said. "After what you've seen, anyone would be a bit unnerved."

"What?" I said in surprise.

I was met with incredulous looks again. Neilson and Stormy eyed one another.

"The hand, Ma'am. "Neilson said.

Of course. He didn't mean my vision. He meant the damn bloody hand. "Oh, yes. It's very disturbing," I hurried on.

***

Another hour later, I was finally back in my car. It felt like I'd been grilled longer than a frozen piece of chicken breast. They asked me question after question before deciding if they were satisfied with my lack of knowledge. My rocky beginning of the interview clearly increased their desire to question me. What's a girl to do? It's not every day you shake a hand and see a grisly murder scene appear before your eyes.

Here's how I look at it, I typically see things for one of two reasons: either it has to do with someone I'm near, or it's something I'm supposed to try and change. The real question is why shaking Neilson's hand was the trigger. He could be the killer. He could be the victim. Or it could be someone he knows. As far as if I'm supposed to try and change it, I have no idea, but I don't want to touch this with a twenty-foot pole. The last thing I need is to garner more unwanted attention from the police after I pulled that little light shenanigan at the lake and hiking trail.

I threw my car in reverse and started backing up. Crunch. Well, if today isn't shit on a stick then I don't know what is. I put my car back in park, turned it off, and jumped out to see whose car I'd backed in to.

Officer Stormy. Great. He was out and looking more humored than he should for someone who had just been backed into by the person they'd been interrogating for the last hour.

"Oh God! I'm so sorry!" I began, but he interrupted.

"Nothing but a little scratch and dent. Let's swap insurance and go on our way."

As we swapped information, he gave me his cell phone number, and asked for mine. I reciprocated. I got back in my car and backed out very carefully this time around. By the time I pulled up in my driveway, I could hear my dog yowling at me frantically.

You see, Ozzie and I could talk. I don't mean he talks out loud, but rather I can hear his thoughts and he mine. I mean I can easily read most people's thoughts, so it makes sense, despite people not believing it, that animals have complex thoughts too. My dog is one smart little booger.

Before my front door was unlocked, he was yelling at me.

"Mom! Mom! Mom! I'm so hungry! I have to pee! I'm so glad you came home!"

I started soothing him as I unlocked his crate and put him on the leash. He hates being home alone, so it makes him super happy to see me if I've been gone a few hours. He lays on the guilt like frosting on a cake when I crate him instead of leaving him to roam. Too bad he likes to eat all my nice things.

A little later after we'd settled in on the couch together, Ozzie said, "Did your friend find you, Mama?"

"What do you mean Oz Man?"

"The nice man that came by asked me where you were!"

And at the precise moment, the ghost from earlier today walked right through my front door. Well, flippin' flapjack. Today really wasn't my day.

Chapter 3

To be honest, I'm usually a very empathetic person, but ghosts just aren't my cup of tea. They always freak out about being dead, and they never know why they didn't cross right on over. Once they realize they're dead, they get all mad about you still being alive. I just hate the tantrum that always ensues. I know I should want to help them, but most of them are just jerks. I guess waking up dead would do that to a person.

This guy here, he was something else. He wasn't just pissed off. He was livid at me because of earlier. To be fair, I wasn't super nice to him. I guess I was dealing with my own demons.

"Lady, if I'm dead, why the hell can you see me?"

"Well, I can see ghosts."

"You're cracked up. Ghosts aren't real, Lady. What type of sick joke do you think this is?"

"It's no joke."

We looked at each other, sizing up the other one. Here's the problem, ghosts don't look like they're dead from whatever killed them. They look fine. I mean a little translucent, but pretty normal otherwise. This guy could be the hand guy. This guy could be the murdered on the floor guy. I don't know. They could be the same guy. They were probably about the same age and build, but let's face it, it's not easy to focus on details when you see a flash of a grisly murder scene. It's also not easy to tell a dead guy from a decapitated hand.

Another problem with ghosts are that they rarely remember dying until they've been dead quite a while. It's like they go blackout drunk. You really have to handle them with care, or they get belligerent, also like a drunk. This guy was well on the way.

The best and maybe only good part about new ghosts: they tend to disappear when they get angry. They don't know how to control their energy, and they just pop up places. They also just pop away.

This guy was about ten seconds away from poof goes the ghost.

He started again, "Lady, I swear to God if you don't tell me what's going on, I'm gonna..."

And poof. He was gone. At least he didn't get to finish that threat. Doesn't seem like a great idea to threaten people when you are about to cross over to somewhere. Probably don't want to add bad marks to the big book.

At some point, I'd stood up, and now I collapsed back on the couch. I turned to Ozzie and said, "Oz, we're royally screwed."

"Mama, he seemed mean. I don't think we want to be his friend. He was nicer to me earlier than he was to you now."

"No joke, bud. No joke," I said as I covered my face with my hands.

***

Sometime later, I awoke on my couch to the sound of Ozzie barking loudly at my front door. As I looked around the room, I was amazed that Ozzie didn't appear to have eaten anything. I tried to stand up, but the room swam around me. Great, I had a migraine causing a severe bout of vertigo.

As I staggered to my door, I squinted through the peephole, and I saw Officer Stormy standing at my door. He was in plain clothes, though, not his uniform. My dog was furiously growling now. He did not like strangers one little bit. I scooped him up and placed him in his crate. I staggered back to the door, and I opened it.

"Hey, there. I hope you don't mind me stopping by, but it seems you've had a bad day. I thought I'd see if you wanted me to pop that dent out of your back bumper."

For a few seconds, I just stood there staring at him. Then my manners recovered themselves.

"Please come in. Can I get you a drink?"

As he entered, cue loud barking again from my fiercest protector, little sausage dog Ozzie.

"Sure. Water would be fine. Easy little guy."

Before I could say anything, he walked the few steps over and plunged his hand into the crate.

Oz snapped, and blood spurted from Stormy's finger.

"Son of bitch," he swore. "What's he so pissed off for?"

"So sorry, he hates strangers. It takes him time to warm up. Let me clean that and grab his shot records."

"No, no, it's fine. Can I just get a rag? I know better than to shove my hand in with a crate dog that's growling. I guess I had a pretty long day too."

I quickly crossed to my kitchen and pulled a dark red rag out from a drawer. I wet it with cool water and returned to him. By now he'd sat down and was trying to talk to Ozzie.

"Look here, little guy, I'm not trying to hurt you. Can't we be friends?"

Much to my immense surprise, Ozzie rubbed his body against the side of the crate the way he does when he wants a scratch from someone he likes.

I said, "Officer Stormy, your rag."

He turned, "Thank you."

I said, "I think he wants you to pet him now."

"Oh, please call me Calvin,"

He took the rag from me and wrapped his finger in it. With his other hand, he reached out and gently stroked

Ozzie's side. Much to my surprise, Ozzie stayed perfectly still. And that's the moment I knew that Calvin Stormy was a good guy. I always trust my dog's opinion of strangers.

Chapter 4

Last night Calvin popped the dent out of my bumper and my car was good as new. This morning, I discovered my pretty little black car spray painted with red paint. It said BITCH across the driver's side. I didn't really know what to do about it, so I hopped in and drove down to the police station. You could say I gathered a lot of attention as drove downtown and parked in the accessible parking by the door. Today, I needed my cane. My dizziness upon standing was bad enough; I didn't trust my body to go without it.

When I got out of the car, I looked up and saw Calvin walking out the front door of the station. He waved, turned my way, and walked over to see me.

"Hey, stranger! Back into someone again?"

His eyes only barely scanned the cane I was leaning on. Impressive. Normally, I get a definite acknowledgment. The night before, he had noted it leaned by my door. We spoke briefly about my dizziness when he had seen me stumbled.

"No, but I do have a problem," I said. "Take a look at the driver's side."

He strolled around and swore loudly. "Damnit. Do you know who did this?"

"Nope. No idea."

"Well, let's get you inside to file a report. It almost feels connected to you stumbling across stuff yesterday."

"You think? It seems a little random to me," I replied.

"Well, I can't imagine your job angers too many people. Have you had any confrontations with lakes or tress?" he joked.

"You know I photograph people too, right?" I laughed.

"No, I didn't. Your camera was filled with nature shots."

"You looked through the entire thing?"

"Yeah," he said, kind of embarrassed like. "They were really good pictures. You're quite talented."

I rolled my eyes and walked toward the station door. "Let's get this over with," I called over my shoulder.

We strolled through the station to Calvin's desk. He got me a bottle of water and pulled out a notebook.

"Tell me when you discovered this. Start from the very beginning."

"Well, I walked outside to walk my dog. As Ozzie was peeing on the tire, I looked up and saw the bright red spray paint. I stood there for a few minutes contemplating what to do, and then I took him in and crated him. Then, I drove here."

"Did you stop anywhere on the way?"

"No. Why?"

"Your hair doesn't look brushed."

My God. I hadn't touched my hair before I left. I changed out of my chewed on sneakers and walked right out the door. "Flip on a stick! I got so caught up that I didn't touch it," I said self-consciously.

He grinned showing all of his pearly whites. Damn, his eye crinkles were pretty cute too.

"No worries. I'll leave that out of the report," he joked.

Was he flirting with me? Was this just who he was? God, I'm helpless at the flirty flirty thing. So sometimes I'm bit socially awkward. I shrugged at him a little frustrated.

We finished filing the report within about five minutes. As I stood to leave, he asked, "You want to grab dinner tonight?"

Holy amazeballs. This man was crazy. I'd been nothing but trouble since he met me. He was probably just asking to be nice. I'm sure he didn't like me. I clearly hesitated too long because he said, "Forget it. Sorry."

"No, no! I'd love to," I drawled out in my anxious southern accent. When I get nervous, I always sound like I'm from the Deep South, not the Midwest.

"Oh cool..." he added awkwardly. "I'll call you when I get off at five."

I tried to walk away confidently, but the damn cane made that more difficult. When I got outside, I got in my car and drove home thinking all about tonight's dinner plans.

The day drug on. I was anxious for some reason. I washed my hair, painted my nails, and put on some makeup for once. Then, I paced around, feeling all nervous. It had been a while since I'd been on any sort of date.

Five o'clock came and went. Then six came and went. By seven, I was drinking wine at my table while my dog and I ate chicken nuggets. I knew what happened. I had been stood up. It's not the first time this has happened to me, and I was sure it wouldn't be the last time either.

I heard a knock at my door at around 7:30. I staggered to it and peeked through the peephole. Calvin. What the hell? I opened the door, trying not to look drunk. He looked at me with a confused look.

"Why didn't you answer your phone? I was worried."

"I didn't get any calls. I thought you weren't coming."

"I've called six times."

Without waiting for an invitation, he stepped past me into the living room. I picked up my phone. No signal. Mother Flipper. I turned to him and held up the phone.

"I guess I had no signal. There's a dead zone here. Sometimes it doesn't ring."

He watched me for a second, and then he was staring at my wine and nuggets. "Mind if I join you?" he asked.

"Be my guest," I said as Ozzie charged over and jumped in Calvin's lap as he sat down at the table. I pulled out another glass and poured him some wine.

Chapter 5

Calvin left around midnight. We drank two bottles of wine and ordered a pizza because Ozzie made off with most of the nuggets. Oz is a persistent little guy. Calvin and I had sat on the couch and watched some random horror movie that was on tv. Really, we spent more time talking than watching.

I normally had a hard time talking to people I didn't know well. I wasn't the best conversationist but talking to Calvin was as natural as breathing. I felt like i'd known him way longer than I had.

As he left, he turned to me and said, "Call Larry at the detail shop about your car. He's on Main Street. He's got the best prices in town. Tell him I sent you. He's a good friend of mine."

Then, he leaned in. He was going for a hug. I awkwardly leaned in too much and headbutted him on the chin. Smooth, Reba. Super smooth.

He grabbed his chin in surprise but laughed instead of looking annoyed. I mean, I wouldn't have blamed him, I'd bonked him pretty dang hard.

As he strolled off, he called back quietly over his shoulder, "I still owe you dinner. Call you tomorrow. "

I closed my door and locked it. I staggered to the bathroom and undressed. I crawled right in the shower. As the hot water sobered me, I heard Ozzie barking loudly in the other room. I figured it was just a neighbor making noise. Ozzie would bark at his own butt, so it didn't actually make me worry to hear him raising cane. A few minutes later, he started barking again. I got out and wrapped my favorite plush towel around me to go check on him.

I left water dripping all over the floor as I walked into my living room. I'd have to clean it up in a few minutes. As I crossed towards the door, I saw a shape moving outside my window. I froze. Who could it be?

Ozzie was furious. He was growling and barking like I'd only heard a few times in his life. None of those times had been because of good things. Once a drunk man had staggered into my unlocked house. Another time was when Ozzie had accompanied me to the park, and a guy grabbed my butt. The most memorable time had been when my ex slapped me across the face when I broke up with him. Ozzie was a fierce little protector. He'd take out an ankle artery if he needed to.

As I backed away towards my room where my phone and clothes were, a brick came crashing through my window, missing me by mere inches. Ozzie lost his utter shit. I scooped him up, so he didn't get cut by the glass all over my floor. I ran back to my bedroom. I shut and locked the door.

I grabbed sweatpants and a t-shirt and yanked them over my wet body. I went into my closet and grabbed my baseball bat. I don't own a gun. I don't like them, so all I could do was wait with my bat.

Minutes ticked by, and I heard nothing. My phone rang. I about jumped out of my skin. I grabbed it and answered Calvin.

"Hello?"

"Are you okay? I just heard over the scanner that there is a disturbance reported at your place. They said they'd received no answer at the door."

"I'm in the back of the house. Someone threw a brick through my window."

"Neilson is there. Go open the door. I'm on the way back."

Now I had two choices here. I could say I don't trust Neilson because I had a voodoo vision when I shook his hand, or I could go open my damn door.

I chose option B. The only thing nagging me is that I never heard a knock on my door. When I opened the door, Neilson was standing there.

He said, "Reba, a neighbor called in a disturbance. I knocked, but I didn't hear anything but a barking dog. Then I noticed the window was broke."

"When the brick was thrown through the window, I took my dog to the back where I keep a bat for protection. We were hiding."

"A bat?"

"Yeah, like a slugger," I said.

He rolled his eyes. "Well, that wouldn't have helped much if they had a gun..."

"Well, I don't own a gun," I said haughtily. "I don't even like them."

Right then, I heard a loud crash from the back of the house. I took off that way, and Neilson followed, drawing his gun. I swung the door open to my bedroom to find Ozzie on the floor under my flatscreen tv he knocked off on him. Damn. He must have been messing with the cord again. I yanked it off him, and he soared right at Neilson growling loudly. Luckily Neilson jumped back, and he was wearing good boots.

Before I could do more than call out Ozzie's name, Calvin came right through the door of my bedroom and grabbed Ozzie up. Ozzie calmed immediately and started licking him.

Neilson looked surprised. He said, "What are you doing here Stormy?" he said.

"I heard about the disturbance, and I called her. I'd only left a little while ago, so I came back."

"Wait, you were here?"

"Oh yeah, we were watching a movie and having pizza," I said.

The room was awkwardly tense and silent. Clearly, Neilson disapproved. He motioned for us to go back to the living room. I crated Ozzie for Neilson's protection.

By now, other officers had arrived. The next hour was loud (Ozzie barking) and stressful (me giving statements). I had questions slung at me, and they wanted a list of any person who might be mad at me. I couldn't really think of anyone recently, but they made me think back over several months. I came up with a list of four people. I didn't think any of them were the person though.

After the officers left, Calvin asked me if I wanted him to stay. At first, I said no, but then I got nervous. He could tell.

He said, "Look, just throw a blanket on the couch. I'll crash here for tonight. Tomorrow we will find out who did this, and then I can get out of your hair."

"Thank you," I said as I went to retrieve a blanket and spare pillow. "Otherwise, I probably wouldn't sleep a wink."

He smiled at me encouragingly, and that's when I got a flash of him covered in blood at the feet of Neilson who was holding a gun.

Chapter 6

This flash left me in quite a pickle. It wasn't an easy predicament. How was I to tell Calvin that I thought his boss was going to try and kill him? How was I to explain anything without telling him about my abilities and making him think I was a crazy?

I drug my feet gathering the blanket and pillow from my linen closet. I was about to hyperventilate by the time I walked back to where Calvin was waiting in the living room. He was seated on the couch, patiently waiting. He took the blanket and pillow from me.

I decided to dive right in. I said, "I need to tell you something, but it's going to be weird. You might think I'm crazy, but I still have to tell you."

He raised his eyebrows and said, "I doubt you could make me think you were crazy. Tell me what's on your mind."

I hesitated a moment, biding my time, but then I decided I was all or nothing. I said, "I think Neilson is going to try and kill you."

His eyebrows about shot off his forehead. His face broke out in a grin. Now, he was just pissing me off. It wasn't funny. I was trying to save his stupid life.

"Hey, now! I'm not joking. Call me crazy if you want, but I've seen some funny things," I said angrily. I felt my face getting hot. My eyes were filling with tears. Great. I hate being an angry crier. People always think you're going to dissolve when in reality, you want to kill them.

"Whoa there, Reba! I'm not laughing at you. I'm just saying that's doubtful. What do you mean you've seen some things?"

I tried to take deep calm breaths as I stood there glaring at him. "I mean I see things I can't exactly explain, like when I accidentally made that light blow up. I can do things, see things, that don't always make logical sense. I know you probably think I need to see a shrink, but I've done this for a few years. Well, really, I've done it my whole life."

He said nothing for a few seconds. Then, he said, "Sometimes I see things too. Sometimes I hear things as well. Things that I can't explain. Things that made me want to be a cop so I could help people. I've seen things that scared me. I do believe you, but I just don't think Neilson is a killer."

Well, that was much easier than I thought it would be. I felt my posture and face drain of the anger I had been feeling seconds before. He really believed me. Holy cow! He actually truly believed me. That was a first.

"Look, when I touched Neilson the first time, I saw a flash of a dead person on the floor. Then, he never knocked on my door. I would have heard. A minute ago I got a flash of you at Neilson's feet, all bloody, and him holding a gun while standing above you. I don't know what it means, but I do know that I don't want to find out with you dead."

His face was pensive, but also serious. I could tell he was contemplating what I'd just told him. "Well, I don't know what that means, but I do know that now that I know, I will be really careful. Have you ever told anyone else about your..."

"Abilities? Not since I was a teenager and someone I told informed the entire cafeteria. People called me Crazy Reba for months."

He cringed and replied, "Yeah, I get that. Thank you for trusting me. I've never told anyone. Ever. I was afraid they'd think I was absolutely crazy. It isn't really dinner time conversation for most."

"I know what you mean. It's hard to explain, and it's even harder to know who you can trust." Tears drained down my face as I felt relief spreading through every inch of my body.

Calvin stepped forward and brushed away one of the tears dripping down my face. He looked at me with a look of tenderness.

"You know, I cry when I'm angry," I breathed out.

You know that old cliche of being able to cut the tension with a knife? Yeah, well that fit as we stood there close together looking into each other's eyes. Steam was practically rising from our skin. As Calvin leaned in to kiss me, Ozzie peed on our feet.

Well, that's one way to ruin the moment. We jerked apart before our lips even touched. I squealed in disgust and Calvin guffawed with laughter.

"Guess he doesn't want to share you," he joked.

I said, "Ozzie! What the hell?"

He wagged his little butt, "Because he was touching you. I didn't like it," Oz said as he pranced off.

Calvin looked at me and said, "Can you hear all animals or just Ozzie? Because he's the only one I've ever heard."

"Oh, I can hear them all," I said.

Chapter 7

Calvin helped me clean up the mess on the carpet, and then he made the couch up. I retired to my bedroom. I had a most unpleasant night. I didn't sleep. I kept sneaking into the main part of my house to check on Calvin, and every single noise alarmed me. When six o'clock came round, I rolled out of bed and got dressed. I had an 8:30 maternity photo shoot with a very pregnant client. I went into the kitchen to find that Calvin was already up.

"Morning," I said.

"Morning." Then there was blissful silence. No awkward small talk. Nothing. I poured a bowl of cereal and passed him a bowl. He poured a bowl too.

Then, we ate. A while passed in the pureness of morning silence before he said, "How did you sleep?"

"Not well," I admitted.

"I'm sorry. I was hoping me being here would help you sleep better."

"Oh, I have terrible insomnia," I said. This wasn't a lie, but I also didn't think it was my insomnia keeping me up last night. It was the brick. It was the hand. It was the dead on the floor guy. It was the dead on the floor Calvin.

"Are you all right?" he asked as casually as he could. "You seem off this morning."

"I'm fine," I said a little stiffly.

"Okay, I just thought, you know, you might be stressed or have thought about the brick and came up with a person you think might have done it."

I sighed loudly. I had already told him that I thought Neilson was the one that did it, but there was no need to beat it to death. He likes Neilson, respects him even. Calvin just couldn't believe that he could be a bad guy. I get it. No one wants to believe that someone they trust and admire could be bad news, but I don't trust or like Neilson.

"I think I'm just a little tired. That's all," I lied.

"Well, if you think of anything today, call me. Okay?"

"Sure. I have a photoshoot that should keep me busy this morning. Then, I have to run a few errands later today. I'll be fine."

"If I hear anything, I'll let you know."

Shortly later, Calvin left so he could go and get ready for work. I did the dishes and gathered my supplies. When I went to walk Ozzie, I found him eating my brand-spankin' new tennis shoes. Great. I must have forgotten to pick them up out off the floor. There went $50 I didn't have to waste.

I fussed him down, gave him a nice long walk, and put him in his crate before I left. When I went to get in my car, I remembered the nasty word written on the side. I decided to stop by the detail shop on my way to the park I was doing pictures at. I was, as usual, running quite early.

When I pulled up, I hopped out and ask for Larry. He came out front to meet me. We hashed out all the details, and much to my surprise, he offered me a loaner and to get me fixed up within two business days. I asked how much the loaner was and once again was surprised at it being complimentary. Now, that's good service!

As he walked me out to get in the little red car he was loaning me, I noticed Neilson parked across the way. How odd? Shouldn't the chief of police have better things to do than trail me around?

I got in my little loaner and drove away. I noticed Neilson tailing me. Well, that was a problem, but at least I didn't have to go to my photo shoot with a car that screamed unprofessional. I drove slowly and meticulously across town. Driving a vehicle that wasn't mine made me nervous. Neilson was still in tow when I got to the park. I pulled in and waited until I saw my client pull up to get out of my car.

***

The day proceeded uneventfully from there. By the time I finished up with my client, Neilson was nowhere to be seen. I went shopping for new shoes, paid some bills, and went and bought groceries. When I got back home, Ozzie was in a real tizzy though.

Mr. Ghost Man had apparently been hanging out for a while. I guess Oz wasn't a big fan. Ghost Man and I did the whole staring contest thing. He looked. I looked. Then he said, "I can't believe I'm dead. I could kill that asshole."

I don't know why, but I laughed. It was a bad idea. He charged at me. I fell over trying to move and hit my head on the coffee table. That was going to hurt like heck later.

"Freakin' A! Calm down. I just don't think you need to be threatening people when you know, you're going to have to be going before the big man soon, that's all. "

"I'm an atheist!" he spat at me.

"Okay! Say what ya want then, but I don't know what you keep coming around for."

"No one else seems to be able to see me except you and some guy by the liquor store."

Then he was gone. Damn ghost. I wanted to know more about who else had been able to see him. That brief conversation was a flat waste of my time. The only way I like talking to a ghost is if they can give me useful information.

I brought in my groceries from the car and walked my dog. Ozzie excitedly sniffed my new shoes while I glared at him. I needed to do some good old fashion baking to make me feel better. As I dug around in my cabinets to see if I had enough supplies to make the cookies I wanted, I couldn't help but think about Neilson. If he wasn't a bad guy, aka murderer, then who was the killer? There had been too much drama.

Luckily, I had everything I needed for my cookies at least. I read through my recipe.

Flourless Peanut Butter Cookies

Ingredients:

1 cup peanut butter

1 cup white sugar

1 large egg

1 teaspoon baking soda

1/2 cup chocolate chips

Instructions:

1. Preheat the oven to 350F. Line 2 cookie sheets with parchment.

2. In a large bowl stir together the peanut butter, sugar, egg & baking soda and evenly combined.

3. Stir in the chocolate chips.

4. Form into balls about 1 tablespoon in size and place 2 inches apart on the lined cookie sheets.

5. Bake for 10 minutes or until the tops look set.

Yields: 18 large cookies

Perfect. This is what I needed to feel better. Twenty minutes later, I was pulling the cookies out of the oven, and my house smelled so delicious I could have eaten it! You see, I like to bake or cook when I'm stressed. Okay, fine I want to eat baked goods or good cooking when I'm stressed. Since I don't have a maid, it leaves me to do the hard work.

I sampled a few cookies before they cooled. Yummy! They'd turned out perfect. I went to the other part of the house to change into comfy clothes so I could edit this morning's pictures. I heard a knock at the door, and I went to open it. There stood Neilson.

Chapter 8

I know what you are thinking right now. What type of absolute crazy person lets someone they think might be a murderer into their house when they are home alone? Well, I needed to get another flash. So, I danced with the devil and offered that bugger a cookie. He accepted it. Now, I'd crated Ozzie before I let him in this time. We did not need him deciding to go a little gremlin on him and nicking an ankle artery or something.

As he settled in, he told me he had a few questions he needed to ask me. Since I didn't feel like I had much of choice in the matter, I told him of course.

He waited for me to get all settled in at the table before he asked if I knew I'd been followed earlier today.

I replied, "Well, yes, you were following me."

He laughed. "Reba, I meant by the green SUV. I was tailing a suspect in the possible murder case you accidentally photographed. Then, I realized he was tailing you."

"Why were you tailing him? Shouldn't someone else get that job?"

"I actually enjoy fieldwork. Did you know he was tailing you?"

"No," I admitted.

"Well, I wonder if he was interrupted by you the day of your unfortunate discovery. Now I'm afraid you could be in serious danger."

"Why would anyone want to hurt me?"

"You photographed a crime scene by accident. That makes you a key witness," he replied.

Well, that hit me like a ton of bricks. This murderer could think I have evidence that could put him away. I'd stumbled into the middle of one of my worst nightmares. I was the potential target of a crazed murderer.

You see, three years earlier, my best friend was murdered. She took a trip to visit a friend from college, and while there, they went clubbing. She got pretty drunk and stumbled out to get a cab. She saw a man stab a woman in the back alley. She yelled and hurried over to try and save the woman, but she couldn't. She stayed a few extra days with her friend to talk with the police about things she saw, but the night before she was due to come home, she was killed. She and her friend went for a walk together around sunset. The man had been watching her, but she didn't realize it. He shot and killed her. Luckily her friend got a good enough look that they caught him two weeks later, but it didn't save Kate. She is gone forever.

I've had nightmares about it over and over since then. I was supposed to go with her on that trip, but I'd been feeling ill. I always wonder if things would have turned out differently had I been there. Anytime I think about it, I dream I'm at her funeral. Now I'm living the hell of being an unintentional victim myself. What if I become the target of a killer because my photos could help put them away? I started feeling the room swim around me. I didn't know if Neilson was trouble, but I did know that I'd gotten myself into a world of hurt all because I'd listened to my gut which directed me out to the lake and hiking trails that morning. I'd put myself in jeopardy because of listening to that little voice in my head. I knew better. I should have stayed the hell away.

After a couple moments of silence, Neilson spoke. He said, "Look, we are going to provide you with protection. It's going to be okay, but I think that we need your help. I want you to look back through the photos you took and see if you notice anything else that might be out of the ordinary. How often do you visit the lake and the trail?"

"Often," I admitted. "I like to go there when I'm stressed out. It helps me feel centered." "Well then, you might see if there is anything out of place. We've combed the pictures carefully, but this guy was careful. It appears that the hand may have been removed prior to killing the victim. Hell, we don't even know if the victim is a victim of murder or if they could be seriously injured somewhere being held captive."

That was more than I could take. I had to help. The most confusing part is that I'm an empath, and I could tell this was seriously worrying Neilson. Maybe he was one of the good guys after all. I'd have to keep my eye on him.

"I'll help. When should I come in?"

"Can you come now?"

"Yes. I'll meet you there in half an hour."

***

Everything happened really fast after he left. I went and changed clothes. I walked Ozzie and crated him. Then I got too scared to leave him home. What if someone came in and hurt him? So, I called my mom.

"Mom?"

"Yes? How are you today?"

"I'm okay. Could you watch Ozzie for a little while? I can't explain, but I don't want to leave him home alone. I had a break in of sorts last night."

"Oh, God! Yes. Bring him over. Are you both okay?"

"Yes, we are. I just have to go up to the police station, and I don't want to leave him home alone."

"Of course. Bring my grandpup over."

I hung up the phone. Then I got all of his stuff ready. I grabbed some food, his bowl, and his favorite toy. We loaded up in the car, and I drove straight to the north side of Stillwater. When I pulled up, my mom was waiting on her front porch for us. She came out and grabbed his stuff. I walked him inside and gave him all the love. She noted I looked upset.

"Honey, what's wrong?"

"Nothing, Mom. I'm just tired," I lied. I didn't want to scare her.

"No, I know that frown line. I get it when I'm anxious or lying. Tell me what happened." She knew me so well. We're practically the same person.

"I don't have time right now. I will explain after I finish up at the station."

"Okay, be careful, Rosie," she said.

My mom always called me Rosie, and she was the only person that had that right. I smiled as warmly as I could muster, and then I left. As I drove to the police station, I noticed a green SUV tailing me the entire way. I couldn't see the person driving all that well, but the vehicle was never out of sight for more than a few seconds, leading me to believe that I was, for sure, being tailed by someone.

Chapter 9

When I got to the station, Neilson and Calvin were out front talking. Apparently, they were waiting for me to get there. Calvin looked as worried I felt. I pasted a smile to my face and hopped out of my car in what I hoped would be a cheerful and unworried manner. My bubbles and bouncing didn't go too well. My right leg, the one that usually gives me problems, gave out. I went down hard and smacked the pavement.

They both ran towards me. My pride was seriously injured. Luckily, that appeared to be the worst part. I had a small scratch on my arm but was otherwise just mentally dying of embarrassment. They both reached out to helped me up. After I was on my feet, I tried that fake smile thing again. They exchanged a look that rubbed me the wrong way. "What?" I said haughtily.

Calvin replied, "You'd be crazy if you weren't a little scared. You don't have to fake it."

I didn't know what to say. I was really stressed out, but I don't like to show weakness. It's my unfortunate personality quirk. I will fake it so long it makes me look ridiculous.

"I'm fine," I said stiffly.

They shrugged at each other. We went walking in. I saw lots of eyes watching us. You see, stuff happens in Stillwater, but it's normally kept pretty quiet. Clearly, the whole department knew about me coming in to look through photos.

As I passed a desk near Calvin's, I almost squealed with fright. The dead guy, aka Ghost Man, was seated eating a sandwich. How could that be possible?

I forced myself to keep walking despite the knot in my stomach. I took deep calming breaths. How could he be alive? It wasn't possible. Calvin sensed my anxiety, but Neilson asked me to follow him into his office. I did so willingly. I wanted out of the sight of others if I passed out from lack of oxygen.

Calvin followed us in. Neilson offered me some water. I accepted but was taken aback when he opened a cabinet that was hiding a mini fridge. He pulled a glass down from a shelf and poured out of a pitcher. Shit. What if he was really a bad guy? He could be poisoning me.

Neilson turned and eyed me. "Would you stop that?" he said. "I'm not a killer."

I blanched. What the heck? Could he hear me?

"Yes, I can," he replied.

Testing. Testing.

"For God's sake. Cut it out, Miss Parker."

"I'm lost," Calvin said.

"He can hear my thoughts. He also seems to know about my abilities," I said.

"I also got the flash you got when you first met me," Neilson responded. "I still don't know who that man was on the ground."

"Oh my God. Do you know if ghosts can come back to life?"

"What? Of course not," he laughed.

"Well, one of your cops has been visiting me in ghost form."

"Oh, shit. Wilson's twin brother has been missing for two weeks. He thought he ran off with some lady from out of town," Neilson said.

"Which one is Wilson?" I asked.

Calvin pointed to the not-a-ghost-sandwich-guy.

"Yep. I first saw him where the hand was discovered," I said.

They looked at each other with trepidation. Then, Calvin's face contorted in irritation. "You have ability?" he said to Neilson.

Neilson shrugged. "Yeah. I knew you did too, but I wasn't sure that you knew that you had ability. I couldn't just say 'Hey, you can do things most people don't believe in, can't you?' could I now?" Neilson said.

Calvin studied him closely. While he still looked annoyed, his face softened a little. "I guess not," he said gruffly. "But it would have been nice to know that I wasn't a lunatic."

I was waiting as patiently as I could for us to get back to the whole not-dead-guy out there. While Calvin and Neilson stared at each other, I was growing restless. I wanted to do what I came for, or at the very least, I wanted to talk about the ghost that I have been seeing. I mean, I've never really had someone to talk to about this kind of thing.

After a minute or two, I realized that they were talking in their heads. Well, well, well, two can play at that game.

I focused my energy carefully and tore down the wall that I usually kept in place so that I didn't get the thoughts of every person in a mile radius. Taking down my wall is a little like taking legos apart. You do it brick by brick, and sometimes it takes a good prying to make them pop apart. After a few seconds, I could hear them loud and clear.

"Do you think we are putting her in worse danger being here?" asked Calvin.

"No, I think leaving her alone is putting her at more risk," replied Neilson.

"I mean, I know you're right, but I don't want her getting mixed up in a mess that she might not be prepared for."

"I think that ship is long sailed. She accidentally interrupted a murderer at his crime scene. She is in danger already. Let's keep her safe. I'll put you on her."

"Okay, I don't want her left alone at all. I'm not letting her get hurt."

"Guys, I'm listening now. I didn't know that you would be able to do this Calvin."

"I couldn't on my own. It's Neilson."

Well, at least that explained that. "Can we talk out loud, gentleman?"

They laughed. I get the feeling they are friends. They both looked at me. Shit fire and save the matches. I need to rebuild my wall. I don't want them hearing my thoughts so easily. I closed my eyes for a few seconds. I pictured my wall as a lovely spring green. I imagined each brick being slapped into place. Then, I focused on my energy and starting at my feet, centered the energy around each chakra. Much better.

When I opened my eyes, they were looking at me with interest. They must have felt the change in my energy.

Neilson said, "How in Sam's hell, did you do that?"

"I don't know," I admitted. "I learned when I was in high school. I couldn't stand to be around large groups of people, so I figured out that I could shut them out if I tried."

"That's useful," said Neilson.

Calvin grinned with his perfect smile. "Well, plenty of time to keep impressing Neilson later. Let's get you in front of a computer."

Neilson said, "I will want a few lessons, Miss Parker. You are quite impressive for someone who self-trained."

As I was lead from the room, it occurred to me that if I self-trained, then there must be places that actually train people like me. Maybe I'd ask him about that soon.

Chapter 10

I spent the next three hours in front of an old computer looking at my own photos. When I say old, I mean this thing was a freaking dinosaur. Despite the rundown technology, I did find a shot that had a person in it, but they were way off in the distance. I hadn't even noticed them at the time I took the photo. Unfortunately, I think it was a picture of ghost man before he became ghost man. It was one of the first pictures I took. When I told Calvin and Neilson, they said they were going to see if forensics could enhance it enough to get a better look. I was hopeful it would work, but I found it doubtful because I was using a top-notch camera that should have been about as clear as it could get. Also, let's face it, if their forensics had the type of technology I'd been using the last little while, they didn't stand a chance of getting it to look more clear.

When lunchtime came around, Calvin asked me to join him. I obliged, happily. We went and grabbed a sandwich from a cafe down the road and came back to the conference room to eat. He then explained that until some of this was sorted out, he didn't want me to be alone. I told him I needed to call my mom and come clean since she was watching Ozzie for me. He said we could go get him to come to hang out with me if I'd like.

You see, this made me nervous. If I brought him here, he might get nervous and nip someone. He takes time to get to know new strangers, but on the other hand, I wanted to have him with me. He was my little pal, amigo, and essentially my self-trained service dog. We decided to go and get him. As we drove across town to pick him up, I realized it would probably make my mom nervous that I was showing up in a cop car.

Sure enough, my mom looked super anxious when she answered her door.

"Honey, what's going on?"

"Can we come in?" I asked.

"Of course! Where are manners?" she said.

We came inside and settled down on the couch where Oz came over and crawled on my lap. He rolled over and gave me his tummy to scratch. He always loves tummy rubs, but he does it a lot more when he can sense I'm anxious. I had to start somewhere, so I started from the beginning. My mom got paler and paler as I went on. By the time I finished, she looked like a light breeze could blow her right over.

Calvin said, "Mrs. Parker, I promise to take care of your daughter. It will all be just fine."

"Ms. Parker, but please call me Rebecca. Thank you for being so reassuring, but I'm still worried. Rosie, will you please call me and text me to keep me updated. If you need Oz to hang out here, you can bring him anytime you need," she said.

Poor Mom. She was so worried. I could feel it. This is why I hadn't told her. I was sure how concerned it would make her, and I hate stressing her. We are close, and she always worries about me, just like I worry about her.

We gathered up Ozzie and his supplies to head back to the station. I got the spare carrier from my house on the way that way Ozzie would have his own little space. When we got to the station, we went straight to the conference room. Ozzie was weirdly calm. He knew that I needed him to cooperate. After I had settled back in, and Calvin went back to talk to Neilson, Ozzie said, "Mom, I'm sorry I was mean to Officer Neilson."

"Why didn't you like him?" I asked.

"He makes me nervous. His energy is so strong!"

"Bad strong?" I asked.

"No, just strong. It feels like a storm is coming when he's near."

Well, if that wasn't cryptic, I didn't know what was. Before I could ask him more, the door opened, and Neilson walked in with Calvin. Neilson looked a little reluctant to get near little Oz, so I put him in the crate I'd brought. Neilson sat down and said, "So I have a question to ask you. If you don't want to do what I'm going to ask you for, you can say no. If you do, then we can go from there."

"Okay," I responded reluctantly. This didn't sound good to me.

"Do you want to look at the crime scene photos and see if you get a flash of anything?"

I hesitated. Did I want to do that? I wasn't sure. I wanted to help. I wanted all this be over with. I wanted to stop being scared. Well holy guacamole sounds like I knew what my answer was. Too bad my desire to help overpowered my desire to hide my head in the sand.

"Yes, I will do that," I started.

"You don't have to," Calvin said quickly.

Well, we know whose idea this was and whose it wasn't. Clearly, Calvin didn't like the idea, and Neilson did. I wondered why Calvin was against it, but it didn't seem like the moment to ask him. I'd have to do that later.

"I'm fine to look. Bring them to me," I said.

They both left the room. I sat there waiting. When they returned, Calvin looked deeply unhappy. He frowned as he sat the file down in front of me. "Do you want me to stay while you look, or do you want to be alone?" he asked.

"I'd like a few minutes alone if that's all right," I responded.

I control my abilities the best when no one is near me. I can open up properly without risk of colliding with energy that's a little too close for my comfort. I also didn't like the idea of getting stage fright while Calvin stared at me. I needed to be able to focus. As they left the room, I took my wall down brick by brick. Then, I stared at the file. Nothing, so I reached out and opened the file.

Still, nothing happened. I started flipping through the notes and pictures. Then something I'd never experienced before happened. It was like a big family tree was appearing in my mind. The names were in all different colors, yet I instinctively knew what the colors represented. It showed connections between people I didn't even know. The people clearly weren't all related. There were names, symbols, and little pictures. I could tell some people were dead because in my mind's eye I couldn't see their energy. I could tell some people were in danger because of the colors of their energy and the color of their names on the huge chart. It was the most bizarre thing that my energy has ever done. Yet in the middle of everything, my energy was situated. I couldn't see myself, but I could sense myself. I could sense the way my energy reached out and brushed each person on the chart. I could also sense that I was in grave danger. A danger that could mean death if I wasn't careful.

Chapter 11

I sat there for a while before I called Calvin and Neilson into the conference room. When they got in there, I turned my attention to Neilson. "I have a very weird and serious question to ask you," I said. "I didn't get a flash exactly. I got something else that's never happened to me before. When I touched the file, I saw this chart like thing come up in my mind. I could see all these connections between people. Some were alive, and some were dead. It's hard to explain how I know all this, but I do. I have no idea what it was. Have you ever heard of this?"

Neilson looked really shocked. "I do know what that is. It's very, very rare. It's called mind mapping. There aren't that many people in the entire world that can do it. It's one of the rarest and strongest abilities that exist. Was this the first time it's happened to you?"

"Yes," I said.

So you didn't know you could do it?" he asked.

"No, I don't know anything about my abilities. I've self-learned, self-taught, and self-screwed up."

"We could change that," he said. "I know an entire network of people that would help you and support you. All you have to do is say the word. We have to stick together. Our abilities are gifts, but they can get us into trouble."

I was a little hesitant. "Let me think about it. I'm not sure yet if I want people to know."

"That's fine. You know where to find me when you decide," he said. "Did the map help you discover anything?"

"I'm not sure, but Wilson's brother is dead. Also, someone named Gabe is connected to it. I don't get the feeling that he was the killer, though. It's all a little overwhelming. I don't know if I'm getting it all right or not. There is a lot of dark energy around Gabe, though."

Suddenly, I felt exhausted like I'd been working hard all day. My limbs became heavy, my head started to pound, and my eyes felt all droopy like I feel moments before drifting off after a long day of work. Neilson noticed.

"It's the energy drain that looking at the map caused. You need some sugar, caffeine, and to rest for a while. Then you can try looking again. Your energy is like a battery. You can drain it, and then it has to recharge, or it can hurt you. You can't overuse it all at once, especially without training," he explained. "I don't want you trying again right this second. We need to get you to a safe house. I'll put Stormy with you. That way, you will feel comfortable enough to rest."

Everything after that was a blur for a little while. I was shifted out to a car with Oz. They tried to be discrete about it. They took my stuff and Ozzie's cage first. Then, we went. Calvin took me to a house in an area of town I wasn't too familiar with. He helped me inside, and I sat down on the couch. It wasn't long before Ozzie was curled up in my lap, and I was close to dozing off. I'd never felt so tired in my entire life.

***

When I woke up, everything was dark around me. I could feel Ozzie curled up on my legs. A soft blanket was folded over me, and a pillow was behind my head. I was laying like this when I went to sleep. Calvin must have repositioned me. I could feel the leather of the couch against the bottom of my back where my shirt had ridden up. I sat perfectly still in ebony darkness. In the distance, I heard a voice talking to Calvin. I didn't recognize the voice at first, but then I realized it sounded a lot like one of the cops I had heard Calvin speaking with earlier.

"Calvin, you can't let her sleep forever. We should wake her up. She needs to know," said the unfamiliar voice.

"She needs rest. We will not wake her just to stress her out and tell her. It won't help. When she wakes up, I will be the one to tell her. I will be the one to take her back to the station, and I will be the one to comfort her."

"Damnit Calvin, you act like she's your girlfriend. She's just a woman helping with this case that you didn't even know a few days ago."

"She's a lot more than a random woman. If you don't like the way I'm running the show, then see yourself to the damn door, Frank."

I heard whispering, and then I heard someone come into the room with me. They walked to the door, opened it, exited, and shut it behind them. I raised up slowly. My heart was pounding. What did I need to know? What was going to make me upset? Had someone been hurt or killed?

I slowly moved into the kitchen. Calvin was at the table with his laptop.

"Hey," he said as I entered.

"Hey, yourself. What was wrong?"

"Did we wake you? I'm sorry," he said, looking embarrassed. "Frank's a real ass sometimes."

"It was fine. What did you need to tell me?"

"Well, you should probably set down first."

I pulled out the plastic chair and collapsed into it. I wasn't sure I was ready for what I was about to hear. I didn't know if I could take much more bad news.

"A little while ago, we had a man call in and say that his pregnant wife was missing. He was out of town, and when he got home, it looked like she never came home from a photoshoot she had planned with a local photographer. It turns out it was your client."

Everything started spinning around me. My breath was coming in rasps. Oh my God. What if I had put her in danger? What if she and her unborn child were in jeopardy because I needed the money and did the shoot even though my gut said it was a bad idea? I tried to stand up. I needed some air, but my legs were wobbly as a newborn foal. Calvin caught me as I staggered sideways. He left his hands firmly on both my shoulders, and he looked me straight in the eyes.

"Whoa there. We are going to find her. It's going to be okay. I swear to you," he said.

"We have to. How can I help?" I asked. By now, tears were streaming down my face. Man, I'd cried a lot the last couple of days. I couldn't believe what was happening. This couldn't be real. How had my life been turned upside down, practically overnight?

"We can go to the station. Then we can look at everything they know. They have people searching. It's going to be okay," he assured me. "There is no need to worry. She might not have been taken at all. She could have just left. It wouldn't be the first time someone was sure their wife was abducted only to find out she ran off with someone else. Let's hope that's what happened this time."

"It isn't," I said. "All she talked about was how much she wished her husband could have been here, but his business trip didn't allow it. They were struggling with money, so he couldn't reschedule it. She even asked if I would do another shoot in the next couple weeks for a few pictures with him. She was very devoted. She didn't just run off with someone else. That's for sure."

"Well, no matter what, they are looking for her car. They are trying to track her phone. We have all our best men and women on it. We will find her, Reba."

Without a word, I turned away from him. I headed out of the room, and he was right on my heels. We silently gathered our stuff and Ozzie. We went out to get in the car, and I noticed that there was a patrol car headed down the road towards us.

"Who is that?" I asked.

"Our escort. Better safe than sorry," he said.

Chapter 12

We were escorted back to the station. It was all pretty surreal. They honestly thought there was danger enough that Neilson sent two cops to escort me inside in addition to Calvin. What did they think was going to happen? Did they think this guy was waiting to find me? I got a light an airy feeling in the pit of my stomach, which was bad news. That feeling was always reserved for when I was right about something. I'd found out years ago, that sometimes those feelings in the pit of my stomach meant something. If everything felt light and airy, my thought was right. If it felt heavy, then it was wrong. This was foolproof when I got the feeling. He, the murderer, was out there somewhere, and he was waiting for me to be alone. He wanted me.

When we were inside the station, they put me in the conference room again. I noticed that they always had at least one cop within sight of the door like they thought some bad guy was going to come marching inside the station to try and grab me. Ozzie was weirdly accepting of some of the cops. He clearly was a bit unhappy with others. They gave me a copy of the file they were compiling on the missing woman. I'd met her through a social media ad I placed, so I didn't know much about her or her husband. She had seemed kind enough, but the day I met her in person, I'd been a bit distracted. I certainly didn't know her well enough to know if she could have had enemies that targeted her. I was left to assume it had to do with the man that was following me.

I poured over the file much of the night, but nothing. No flashes. No heavy or light and airy feelings. No anything. Until we knew more, they were looking for her car and waiting on forensics in what they hoped was the connecting case with the hand. The first night was the worst of all the nights that followed. Every minute felt like an hour. Every single time I heard a noise, I looked towards the glass-paneled door, praying I'd see someone running in with news. No news came. All I could think about was the statistic about if you don't find a missing person in the first 48, the chances of finding them alive goes down significantly.

When morning came, Neilson entered the conference room. He pulled a chair out across from me at the table and said, "How are you doing, Reba?"

"Awful. My gut told me not to do that photoshoot, but I needed the money. I was broke, so I did it anyway. I put someone in grave danger. I have to learn how to control my ability. I have to start listening to my instincts."

"You can't be so hard on yourself. You've never had training, and to be fair, your instinct could have been telling you that there was a creep following you."

"I just can't imagine how her husband feels. I don't want to know. If I was near him, I'd feel his agony. I'd know how much pain I have caused him." I was just drained. I needed to sleep, to eat, and shower.

"You need to get out of here. I'm going to send Calvin and you to the safe house again. I will have some food sent over. You need to rest. There is nothing else you can do. I promise we have it handled."

I looked at him for a minute. "Can I ask you for a favor?" I asked.

"Of course," he said.

"Can you have someone keep an eye on my mom's house? I went by there multiple times when the guy could have been following me."

"Calvin already has that covered," he said smiling. "He's always one step ahead of the game. He could probably replace me."

"Calvin is great. He's a good one," I said in agreement.

"You know, he's worked here six years. I've never seen him date, but I can tell he's crazy about you."

I looked at him with curiosity. I thought he was completely against there being anything between Calvin and me, but now I sensed he might not disapprove so much.

"He's like a son to me. I want him to be happy," he said almost in response to my thoughts, but this time, he had just sensed more than heard. "I want to see him happy about something other than about work. It's almost unhealthy. He works a lot. When he's on duty and when he's not."

I laughed, "Don't be so sure that I can do that. I'm pretty much a mess. I don't bother dating much anymore. Been burned a few times too many."

"You're too young to give up."

At that moment, Calvin walked into the room. He was wearing a t-shirt and jeans, not his uniform. His broad shoulders were emblazoned against the fabric in a way that made my stomach tighten. It had been a while since I felt that sensation. He made me feel things that I didn't want to feel.

"You ready to go?" he asked.

"Yes. Just let me use the restroom real fast," I said. "Can we go by and get some of my things?"

Neilson cut in, "No, we can send someone to get anything you need." We want you transported in a van with tinted windows. We don't want this guy to know where you are. We want him to come out and start looking. He'll screw up, and we'll nail his ass to the ground when he does."

I sighed. "Okay."

"Here. Make a list," Neilson said as he pushed a piece of paper and a pen over to me. "We'll get someone to get anything you need."

It took me about ten minutes to figure out what all I really wanted and needed brought over. I also needed to put down an approximate location. I felt weird when I put down underwear on the list, but then a young woman came in. She appeared to be around my age or maybe a little younger. She was baby faced, but also looked smart and tough. Her dark brown hair was pulled back in a tight bun on her head that emphasized her pale skin. She smiled at me.

"Hi, my name is Annie. I'm going to be one of the people going to get your things. I thought you might like me to be the one that dug through your clothes and undergarments," she said with a stunning grin that made her look even younger.

I laughed. "Actually, that's a lot better! I was starting to feel weird about some of the things on my list."

"Yeah, no one wants Wilson digging in their panty drawer. The old pervert," she said seriously. Tell me where the stuff is, and I will bring it. If I can't find something, I will give you a call."

"Thanks, Annie. May I ask, how long you've worked here?"

"Sure, I've been here about six months. I really love being in law enforcement, but I'm only twenty-six, so people tend to ask me that question. I look young."

"You'll love that in ten years," I joked.

"Hmm, maybe. In some ways, I think age is a rite of passage. If you don't age, then that means you never had the chance to live. I can't wait to tell the story of every laugh line and wrinkle when I'm old and gray."

I was a little taken aback by her serious response. "I get that, but most people don't," I said.

She laughed. "Sorry for being so serious about that. I'm tired, and I'm really honest when I'm tired."

"That's all right! I'm like that too!" I said with a little more enthusiasm than necessary. "It's really nice to have someone to talk to. I really appreciate your help, Annie."

"Don't mention it! I'm happy to help," she replied.

I finally took my bathroom break. Then, they pulled a van up right by the door. Calvin carried Ozzie and Oz's stuff, and I walked with my things. Before I exited the door, they gave me a hat and sunshades to put on. They were taking this incognito stuff seriously. I was shoved into the van within seconds of exiting into the warm air. They put me in the back so no one could see me, and then they drove away.

Chapter 13

When we got to the safe house, I was ushered inside. All the blinds and curtains were covered and closed. It felt like a prison cell. I was practically being held captive. They brought in the little stuff I had with me. I sat at the table in the kitchen and felt restless while I waited on the breakfast I'd been promised. Neilson came through. An officer dropped by about a half hour after we arrived with eggs, pancakes, bacon, orange juice, coffee, and so much more from the local pancake house.

I ate until I was stuffed, and so did Calvin. We had both filled our stomachs so full we were very sleepy. I was fixing to go get in the shower when Annie came in.

"Watcha doing?" she said while reaching out to snag a leftover piece of bacon.

"I was fixing to get in the shower, so you're just in time," I replied.

"I do my best," she said grinning. Ozzie came running up, wagging his tail. He jumped right into her arms and licked her, much to my ever-present surprise. "I found everything you needed and grabbed a few extra things in case you needed them." She thought tampons loudly at me. "And I got him a couple more toys," she said, scratching Oz on the head.

I jerked when she thought tampons, but she never missed a beat. She grinned. Holy bat wings! She knew about my abilities and had them herself. I tried to focus in on her energy, but my head was hurting too bad. She reached out and patted me. Apparently, I'm not an actual freak. There have been people around my whole life that have abilities like me. Wouldn't that have been nice to know. "Why don't you go grab that shower? I'll wait around for a few."

I thanked her, and I left the room. In the bathroom, I turned the hot water up all the way and just stood under the running water. I scrubbed my body and my hair and then waited for the water to run cold. As the water temperature cooled, goosebumps layered my skin. I sighed out loud. I needed space to let out my emotions. I let the tears fall rapidly and just allowed myself to feel what I needed. Being an empath meant that I had learned to box up overwhelming emotions, but I always paid for it. I had to let them out as soon as possible, or they would completely overwhelm me. The day had been too much.

When the water finally ran ice cold, I got out. I pulled my hair back in a messy wet bun and got dressed. All I needed was some sweatpants and a big t-shirt. Thank goodness I had asked for a sports bra, so I could feel comfortable and covered. I wasted time for a few minutes longer so that I could let my face turn back to normal color. After it looked fine, I left the bathroom to find Calvin and

Annie chatting in the living room. They stopped when I entered.

"What?" I said.

"We were getting worried. It had been awhile," Annie said.

"Oh yeah, sorry. I just needed a few minutes."

"Of course," said Calvin. "You need to get some rest. The bed is all made up. Go ahead. I'll be here if you need me."

I wanted to stay and talk to them, but I was too tired. I gave a shrug, and then I headed to the bedroom and collapsed on the bed.

***

I slept for about three hours. When I woke up, Ozzie was beside me. He was snuggled up to my stomach, but I could feel someone else in the room. I sat up, and I realized that

Calvin had made a pallet on the floor. He looked so youthful while sleeping, but I felt guilty he was on the floor. I quietly stood up and snuck to the kitchen. I was surprised to find Annie reading a book at the table.

"Hey there," I said.

"Hey, yourself. Feel any better after a good rest?"

"Yes, I'm just really overwhelmed," I admitted.

"Well, of course, you are. You didn't sign up for this. You didn't know that one day, your life was going to be turned upside down. You didn't know any of that. It's okay, to be honest about the way you feel."

Once again, I felt interested at her honesty. "Have you always been an empath?" I asked.

"As long as I can remember. My sister was too," she replied.

Was. That was the keyword. I hesitated. "You said was."

"Yeah, she died of cancer two years ago. She was my twin. We were really close. I miss her every single day."

That explained her emphasis on life being a privilege. "I'm sorry," I said, knowing that it sounded empty. "I can't imagine what that must have been like. I lost my best friend not long ago. Well, it was three years, but it still feels like yesterday."

"What happened to her?" she asked.

"She was murdered while on vacation. Saw a crime. The guy decided she was a threat. He killed her," I said emptily. It had been a long time since I'd spoke of this out loud. It was so painful to even think back on.

"That's awful. I bet all this is bringing up old memories. If you need to talk, feel free, but if you don't, that's fine too. I know that sometimes, silence is better than conversation."

I sat down beside her at the table, and we stayed silent. Being near Annie felt like being near a friend, which I needed today, and I wanted to absorb that for a little while longer.

Chapter 14

The next few days were dejecting, to say the least. There was little to no progress, and I felt like I was being held captive. I know they just wanted to keep me safe, but it still felt suffocating. I couldn't walk my dog without at least one armed agent with me. They preferred that I let them walk him, but I couldn't stay stuck in this bland little house all the time.

It was clear that this wasn't home. It was devoid of anything but fearful emotions and crappy furnishings. It had all neutral walls, plastic kitchen dining cutlery, a plastic table and chairs, and most things that looked like they belonged in a sketchy motel off of the interstate. Even Ozzie hated it. It just felt like a temporary resting spot that was only inhabited long enough to find a better option. It felt like being unsettled.

The most significant excursion I had over the next few days was when Calvin took me to change out my loaner car for my freshly painted car. It looked terrific, but I was forced to leave it at the police station as to not draw attention to myself.

During each day, we went to the police station. We stopped on the way in to let Ozzie hang out with my mom. When we got to the station, I helped where I could. I looked through files. I drank a lot of coffee, and I fended off questions from people that wanted to know what my particular set of skills was. People were quite curious about my involvement in such a high-profile case.

Neilson and I discussed what I should say. He said to say that I was a profiler of sorts and that I was trying to make connections between the cases and identify possible suspects. On the upside, some people didn't bother asking. Apparently, it's not uncommon for people in law enforcement to have some sort of ability. They are drawn to the profession. About one third to one half of the force has some type of ability, so those people didn't seem to question my involvement, probably because they could sense me using my energy a lot. I did find that those curious about my involvement were typically uneasy around me as well. It's like they could sense my difference, and they didn't know what it was, so they feared me.

    None of this was helped by the fact that on day one, I used my energy so much that I literally passed out. Neilson and Calvin saw me fall over through the glass paneling of the conference room I was holed up in. Apparently, they came in guns a blazing, thinking I might have been shot through the window. It caused quite a commotion, and I was really embarrassed about it.

Each day, I kept staring at the same old pictures. I kept going through the same old files. I kept examining my map, but nothing stood out more than before. When I tried to get some gut feelings, I couldn't manage much. What I did know for sure was that the ghost guy was Wilson's brother. I knew that my pregnant client and her husband were definitely involved with all of this. I knew that a man named Gabe was connected as well, but my instincts were waffling around. Gabe might or might not be the actual killer, but he had a distinct connection to the case. If he was the killer, his energy was strong enough that it outweighed my instincts.

Wilson seemed to be worrying more about his brother. I overheard him telling Calvin that usually his brother would have called by now. He thought he was hurt or dead. He said he felt it in his gut. Calvin told him it would be okay, but he didn't say too much. He did, after all, know that his brother was indeed dead.

Frank had warmed to me. I even figured out why he didn't like me very much at first. Apparently, Frank and his wife were going through a divorce. She was considerably younger than him, and when she stopped by to give him something, I felt like I was looking at myself. She had the same skin tone, the same hair, and she was about my age. Once Frank realized I was genuinely invested in what I was doing, it seemed he decided to look past my appearances and forgive me for looking much like his soon to be ex-wife.

As the days passed, Annie spent quite a lot of time checking in on me. She often would set with me for a while after her shift or come early. It had been a long time since I had a woman to talk to and just shoot the crap with. Really, it had been since Kate died. Annie and I would chat about random stuff, but it was enough to make me feel better like there was a sense of normalcy in my life.

On the other hand, I never got to forget the fact that all hell was breaking loose for my client's husband. He came by daily. He would come in and ask if they had found her yet. Every single time, he was reminded that they would contact him immediately if they made any progress, but to hang tight in the meantime. They tried to keep me away from him, but I kept trying to get near him.

On day three, I went to get coffee when he was there checking in. He realized who I was, and he asked what I was doing here. I told him I was trying to help find his wife, which he seemed weirdly unsurprised about. I guess he didn't know that I had no law enforcement background. He thanked me profusely.

After that, they told me to stay in the conference room when he was there. They didn't want him asking me questions or telling people I was helping. Calvin and Neilson were extremely strict about it, so I didn't get near him again. I mean, I did try, but they always ushered me away or distracted me the second they saw him coming.

I felt like they had a little information, but they weren't telling me some of the things they knew. Annie, on the other hand, she was forthcoming with information. On day five, there had been a lot of commotion several times, but Neilson and Calvin said it was unrelated. I knew they were lying. When Annie came to chat, she told me they had found the vehicle of Alice, my client, in the ravine on the outskirts of town. There was no body, but they suspected they'd find her soon enough. This was devastating to me, and the guilt was eating me alive. She said that they had told her husband and that he had fallen apart at the seams. I felt truly awful, but she reminded me that it wasn't my fault. I couldn't even tell Calvin and Neilson that I knew because she would have had her ass handed to her on a silver platter.

As the days drug on, I grew more and more restless. All I wanted was some little ray of sunshine. Was that too much to ask for? I was sleeping two or three hours a night on a good night. That was all I ever managed when I was this stressed. Insomnia seemed to be my punishment. My body was acting up. I was keeping a constant migraine. I was aching and using my cane more than normal. My body was on the verge of a full breakdown.

Chapter 15

On day six, I'd had more than I could take. I broke down and sobbed in the conference room. I didn't care if people could see. I couldn't help it. I was exhausted, and all I'd managed to do for the last day or two was get myself so tired I couldn't block out the thoughts of all the traffic in and out of the station. It felt like my brain was on fire from sensory overload. Some of the cops were getting suspicious of my involvement. They'd started thinking nasty things about me, my cane, and a couple wondered if I was the killer. None of this helped me feel any better.

When the tears started, Calvin, Neilson, and Annie came hurrying in. Calvin pulled a chair up beside me and put his arms around me. He patted me while Neilson was looking concerned.

Annie was the first to speak. "I think you need a break. You need to get away from this bleak conference room. You need some fresh air. You need to stop thinking about the case for a few hours," she said.

Neilson added, "I think she's right. You need to get out of here. Why don't you and Stormy go get some dinner. It's on me."

"No, I've got it," Calvin insisted.

It wasn't but a few minutes later that we headed out of the station. We got in his car, not some huge tinted windowed van, and we drove downtown to the little wine bar cafe that had delicious food and a fantastic selection of wine. Once we were settled in, the waitress took our order. We ordered a bottle of wine to share and chicken parmesan with spaghetti for dinner.

When the food arrived, we ate and drank happily. I was so elated that I almost forgot about everything that was stressing me. The wine loosened my nerves, and I kept touching Calvin's hand that was on the table. I felt bold, which wasn't normal for me. By the time we ordered dessert, he was gently holding my hand, rubbing his fingers back and forth over my palm causing goosebumps on my arm. I felt things I hadn't felt in a really long time, but I couldn't bother worrying about that right now.

When we left, we strolled in the warm evening air. It smelled warm and sweet with the coming rain. Right as we got near the car, the heavens opened up, and rain drenched us. We laughed as we climbed into the car dripping with rain.

Calvin drove back to the safe house. I didn't want to go back. I wanted to go home. I wanted to crawl in my bed. I wanted to invite Calvin to my bed. I wanted to forget everything that was weighing me down, but I couldn't. When we pulled up in the driveway, I realized there was no one there except us. Calvin looked at me. He, too, had noted the absence of other people.

We went inside. I excused myself to the bedroom to change into dry clothes. I'd been in there for a couple minutes when I knocked my metal water bottle off the bedside table when I pulled my sticky wet shirt off. The sound reverberated in the quiet. The door swung open, and Calvin rushed in. He must have thought someone was in the room.

There was an absolute recognition between us that I was standing there in my slacks and lace bra. The room went from cold to a fiery inferno in seconds flat. I took the first step towards him. He met me in the middle. He leaned down and kissed me, fingers laced through my damp hair, and I felt every inch of me melt. His chest pressed against mine, which made my nipples stand taut, and that wasn't the only thing standing at attention in this room. He caressed my bare back as his tongue moved into my mouth.

We moved backward and fell onto the bed. His weight pressed down on me, but in a gentle way. We were nothing but a tangle of limbs, hands hungrily exploring each other's bodies like hormonal teenagers in a backseat of a family Buick. I pulled his shirt off, and he unclasped my bra. His mouth trailed down my neck to my breasts. I let out a moan as his fingers trailed down my sides.

We didn't hear Annie let herself in, but I heard her gasp. We had been the only ones there, so the door was wide a jar to the bedroom. She had just seen quite an intimate moment.

We pulled apart quickly. I grabbed my t-shirt, but she had already backed away out of the room. We looked at each awkwardly as we headed to follow her. She was on the couch, face in hands, laughing. Cute.

"Sorry," I said.

She grinned. "No, you are not. You're annoyed. I don't blame you guys. I'm so sorry. I should have knocked."

"You're fine," Calvin said, slightly stiffly. "Is everything okay?

"Yes, I was just making sure you guys made it here, okay. Clearly, you all had a fine time at dinner," she joked.

I gave her a mean look, but she continued to laugh. Eventually, we were all laughing. It was as marvelous an evening as I could have imagined having—almost. I hadn't felt this lighthearted in days.

Chapter 16

As the night went, we played cards with Annie in the living room. She offered to leave, but we told her she was fine to hang out. I mean, let's face it, the mood was already ruined. I got the feeling that she thought Calvin might take advantage of me while I was tipsy, and she was watching out for me. While that was sweet, I was more than happy to let him take advantage of any part of me he wanted.

As bedtime approached, she finally decided to head out. Once it was down to just us again, he looked at me with a look of hunger. Ozzie had stayed at my mom's tonight, so we were free to do as we pleased without interruption. He walked back up to me, and we kissed. I'm not talking a little peck, I'm talking a toes curled type of kiss that I would have been happy if it never ended, but it did. He bid me off to bed, and I went even if a little forlornly.

I changed my clothes into a spaghetti strap shirt and shorts. I climbed in the big bed. I was hyper-aware of the way that the cheap sheets felt against my skin. Each nubby felt like it was grating me into the overly firm mattress. I felt the weight of the last few days shoving me down. Right before I drifted off to sleep, I felt like every nerve in my body came alive and lit the room around me on fire.

Suddenly I was somewhere else. I was in a room filled with wood. The walls had a deep mahogany rustic paneling on them. The floor was carpeted with dirty beige shag carpet that had seen better days. The back corner of the room held a wood burning stove corroded with rust that looked as if it hadn't seen a good blaze in five or ten years. The carpet against one wall was stained a deep crimson. It looked like someone had tried to clean it up, but they had failed miserably.

It was like I was stuck in one place. I couldn't move. I could only look around the room. Then suddenly, I could hear a voice. It sounded like a door opened behind me, but I couldn't see who came in. I could hear footsteps. I needed to hide!

Wait. The man that entered the room was within sight now. He didn't appear to notice me. He crossed to the kitchenette and opened the refrigerator. He pulled out a can of beer and crossed to the threadbare couch in the middle of the room. He was centimeters from me now. I could see the salt and pepper that speckled his beard and his black hair. I could see his olive skin and the skull tattoo that was emblazoned on his left hand.

I'd seen that tattoo before. Where had it been? I knew who this man was. He pulled out his cellphone as he *popped the tab on his beer. He dialed a number, and then he waited for the person on the other end to answer.*

"Hey. It's Gabe. There's no way that we can pull this off without your truck. Mine's still being cleaned. I need to move the body now. I can only leave the out of order sign up so long before someone will complain."

I couldn't know what was being said on the other end of the phone, but as he turned to look backward, it was like my perspective shifted. I could see a large deep freeze against one wall.

That's it. I knew where I was. I was in the lodge out by the lake and trail. I'd used the bathroom in it a few times over the years, so it was vaguely familiar.

Gabe crossed to the deep freeze. He pulled it open, and I could see it was full. I focused as hard as I could on Gabe's energy, and suddenly, I could see through his eyes. He was gazing down into the deep freeze at its contents.

The deep freeze was filled with body parts. They were placed in bags, but I could see hands. I could see heads. I could see things I'd never wanted to see in my entire life. As he fiddled with one of the bags, I saw the face of one of his victims. Eyes wide open and blank as a marble, a familiar face looked back at me with gray skin. It was the old landscaper for the trail and lake. I'd talked with him tons of times, but I hadn't seen him the last time I was there which was unusual. I thought he must have retired, but now I knew better. He was the first victim. I got a light and airy feeling in the pit of my stomach. The flash I'd seen of a man face down, that had been him. He was murdered by Gabe.

"Yeah, I'm about out of room, though. Don't forget that you said for the money you'd do whatever it took, so figured it out."

Gabe hung up the phone.

I jerked awake in the blackness of the room and rolled towards the trash can by the bed. I heaved until I'd emptied the contents of my stomach.

Chapter 17

I climbed out of bed and walked quietly to the bathroom where I stood in front of the mirror. I looked at my ghostly white complexion. The dark circles under my eyes were so prominent they looked like huge onyx, magenta, and plum bruises. My hair was hanging frizzy with curls. I took the hair band off my wrist and pulled my curls into a tight knotted bun on the base of my neck.

What had I just witnessed? I didn't understand how it happened, but I knew it was real. There were decapitated body parts in a freezer. Gabe was a murderer. He'd killed the nice old man landscaper from the local hiking trail. He'd dismembered him and likely Wilson's brother too. And I could tell them where to find Gabe. I could put him away. I could put myself in more danger. I had also. It was the right thing to do. Maybe I could save Alice before it was too late.

It wasn't safe for the team to go at night. I'd wait until morning to share with Neilson and Calvin. I examined my face one more time before I walked out of the bathroom and headed to the kitchen. As I passed through the living room, I saw Calvin sleeping peacefully on the sofa bed. He was smiling, so clearly, he wasn't dreaming of decapitated bodies. As I passed by, he muttered, "Reba..." under his breath.

I walked on to the kitchen. I'd made them bring groceries over the day before. I needed to cook. It's the only thing that would help. I needed to put my energy into something productive. I needed to see real results. Cooking always helped calm me. What did I have the stuff for? I could make my Nutella Brownies. I could make pancakes. I had bacon. I had eggs. I had salsa. I could make egg muffins with bacon and salsa. I'd make it all. I just needed to gather my recipes from my phone. First, I pulled up the brownies.

2 Ingredient Nutella Brownies

Ingredients:

4 large Eggs

1 cup Nutella

Powdered Sugar (, optional)

Directions:

1. Preheat oven to 350.

2. Line an 8x8 brownie pan with parchment paper; set aside.

3. Place the eggs in your mixer's bowl and beat for 5 to 7 minutes, or until the eggs have tripled in size. This may take up to 10 minutes with a handheld mixer on high.

4. Heat the Nutella in the microwave for 60 seconds.

5. Remove and stir.

6. Slowly pour a stream of the warm Nutella over the eggs, beating until mixture is thoroughly combined.

7. Pour batter into prepared pan and bake for 30 to 35 minutes, or until a toothpick inserted in the middle comes out with very few crumbs.

8. Remove and let completely cool before cutting.

9. Dust with powdered sugar.

10. Cut into bars and serve.

As I gathered the eggs from the fridge and the Nutella, I felt myself calming. I meticulously beat the eggs and Nutella together by hand. The energy it took relieved my nerves. I felt my energy calming back down into a normal pattern.

When I placed the brownies in the preheated oven, I turned my attention to the egg muffins. I dug through the cabinets, looking for a muffin pan. After I found one, I pulled up the recipe to double check myself.

Tex-Mex Avocado Egg Muffins

Ingredients:

5 large whole eggs

5 large egg whites

1/4 cup unsweetened almond milk (or milk of choice)

1 large avocado (pitted & diced)

4 tbsp salsa or pico de galo (a thin salsa that isn't too chunky)

1/2 tsp cumin

1 tsp dried cilantro

1/2 tsp pepper

1/4 tsp salt

Directions:

1. Preheat oven to 375 F. Grease 10 muffin cavities of a muffin pan or spray liberally with cooking spray.

2. In a large mixing bowl, whisk together eggs, eggs whites, milk, cumin, cilantro, pepper, salt, and salsa.

3. Transfer to a 2 cup measuring cup then pour into each cavity 3/4 of the way full. Place one tablespoon of diced avocado on top of each muffin cavities.

4. Bake at 375 F 22-25 minutes until muffins are set. Remove from the oven and cool in the pan 5 minutes prior to removing with a mini spatula and transferring to a wire cooling rack.

5. Store in the refrigerator up to 7 days in an airtight container.

Yields: 10 muffins

    I was missing a few ingredients, but I had all the most important ones. I decided to use whole eggs and dairy free milk. I was missing some spices, but I had salsa and avocados for flavor.

    As I whipped together the ingredients in the bowl, I started smelling the brownies. I checked them, found they were done, and pulled them out to let them cool. I poured the egg mixture into the muffin tins and topped with avocado. I slapped them in the oven.

Then, I turned my attention to the pancakes. I had mixed for this, so it didn't take anything but time. No recipe was needed. I mixed the ingredients together. Then, I pulled out a skillet and poured the batter into it. One pancake at a time, I soothed my anxiety. By the time I finished the batter, I was completely calm. I'd made a pan of brownies, 24 pancakes, and ten egg muffins.

As I started to clean up, I heard a little noise in the living room. I filled the sink and loaded all the dishes into the warm soapy water. I felt a hand on my arm, and I jumped. I felt my energy spike, and as I swung around, I saw Calvin crumple to the ground. Oh, hell's bells. I'd knocked him out.

Chapter 18

I crouched down to the floor immediately. He was limp and lifeless, but he was breathing. I definitely didn't kill him. I raised his head gently and placed it in my lap. I placed my fingers on his temples, and I focused all the energy I could on making his energy more distinct. I'd never done this, but it appeared I had sucked his energy away. I just had to figure out how to put in back where it belonged.

Several minutes went by, and I started to panic. I got up out of the floor, and I went and got my cell phone. I dialed Annie's number. It rang and rang. I hung up and tried again.

"What's wrong?" she said sleepily.

"I think I've killed Calvin," I blurted out. "Or maybe just knocked him out. I didn't mean to. He startled me." I was nearly in a complete frenzy now.

"Whoa! Slow down, Reba. You killed him? What did that motherfucker do you? I'll kill him."

I felt confusion. "What? No, he just walked up behind me. Do you dislike Calvin?"

"Oh, I guess I misunderstood. No, I'm just not overly trusting of men. So, he did nothing but startle you?"

"Yes. I think I knocked him unconscious with my energy."

"Just wait it out. He'll wake up in a few minutes," she said in a soothing voice. "If he isn't awake in an hour, call Neilson. He knows how to wake people up."

I got off the phone with her, and I sat back down on the floor. I didn't know what to do, so I just waited.

Five minutes.

Ten minutes.

Fifteen minutes.

Twenty minutes.

His breathing was more defined now.

Twenty-five minutes.

Thirty minutes. He opened his eyes.

"What the hell happened?" he asked.

"I accidentally knocked you out with my energy. I didn't sense you behind me, and it scared me. Oh God Calvin, I'm so sorry."

Much to my surprise, he laughed. "That would be convenient," he said.

After a few seconds of indignation, I laughed a little. "I guess so. Too bad I didn't know how to wake you up. It's been over half an hour. I was distraught, but Annie said you'd be fine and to wait it out."

"Of course, she did," he said laughing. "She hates men. I swear to God she really does. She probably hoped I'd die."

"Calvin, that's not funny. She didn't want you dead."

"Whatever. Speak for yourself. I've seen the distrust she has. Hard to get her to partner with anyone. Also, her last partner lasted like two days before he quit."

I could tell he suddenly remember that it was the middle of the night, and I had filled the house with food. "Reba, what's wrong? When I woke up, I noticed that you were cooking. It's the middle of the night."

"I was stressed," I said. "I cook when I'm stressed. I made brownies, egg muffins, and pancakes. Do you want some food?" I asked as casually as I could.

"Well, you made enough to feed the entire police force, so yeah, I'll join you. What had you so stressed and jumpy that you knocked me out?"

"Let's eat. I will tell you about something weird that happened. I can't quite explain it, but I had a dream of sorts. It was real, though. You and Neilson are going to need to have all the information I gathered. We have a killer to catch."

He looked both worried and impressed. We sat down at the table and helped ourselves. I loaded my plate with two egg muffins, three pancakes, and a huge brownie. His plate was at least twice that size.

"So, you cook when you are worried?"

"Yes, so does my mom. I guess it's a family trait, you could say."

"Well, tell me what has you all up in a tizzy?"

I debated the best way to go about sharing the information with him. There wasn't really a table appropriate way to tell someone about decapitated limbs in a giant freeze, blood-stained carpet, and weird conversations. Well, I had to try. I reached out and took his hand.

"Let me see if I can show you," I said.

I closed my eyes and focused on my vision.

Suddenly we were somewhere else. We were in a room filled with wood. The walls were a deep mahogany rustic paneling just as I remembered. The floor was carpeted with the same dirty beige shag carpet that had seen better days. The back corner of the room held a wood burning stove that looked as if it hadn't seen a good blaze in five or ten years. The carpet against one wall was stained a deep crimson. It looked just as I remembered.

It was like we were stuck in one place. We couldn't move. We could look around the room more freely than I had been able to before. Suddenly, we could hear a voice. It sounded like a door opened behind us.

Wait. The man that entered the room was within sight now. He didn't appear to notice us, just like before. He crossed to the kitchenette and opened the refrigerator. He pulled out a can of beer and crossed to the threadbare couch in the middle of the room. He was centimeters from me now.

We could see his tattooed hand. He dialed a number, and then he waited for the person on the other end to answer.

"Hey. It's Gabe. There's no way that we can pull this off without your truck. Mine's still being cleaned. I need to move the body now. I can only leave the out of order sign up so long before someone will complain."

We still couldn't know what was being said on the other end of the phone, but as he turned to look backward, it was like our perspective shifted rapidly. We could see the large deep freeze against one wall.

Gabe crossed to the deep freeze. He pulled it open, and we could see it was full. I didn't want to focus on it, but for Calvin, I focused as hard as I could on Gabe's energy. He needed to see everything. Just like before, I could see through Gabe's eyes now. He was gazing down into the deep freeze at its contents.

The deep freeze was filled with body parts. They were placed in bags. There were heads. I could see things I'd never wanted to see again in my entire life. As he fiddled with one of the bags, we saw the face I remembered. His eyes were wide open and blank as a marble. Oh, that familiar face looked back at me with his gray skin.

"Yeah, I'm about out of room, though. Don't forget that you said for the money you'd do whatever it took, so figured it out."

Gabe hung up the phone.

I jerked my energy back. Calvin was pale, but he was looking at me with what looked like fear in his eyes. Now we both knew how dangerous this case was.

"You dreamed that?"

"Yes, but it was so much more than a dream."

"Oh, I know. I wondered who that man..." he trailed off.

"It is the landscaper from out at the lake and trail. I didn't see him last time I was there. I'm positive that we were at the lodge on that property. That's where Gabe is at. That's where the bodies are."

Chapter 19

We sat there looking at one another for a few minutes. The silence of the middle of the night discovery weighed down the air between us. We kept eating but in a much less lighthearted manner. We were solemn. Nothing like decapitation to make you understand the seriousness of a situation.

You see, the thing that's so damn frustrating about premonitions is that they are confusing. I know it seems silly to say that, but just because I have psychic abilities doesn't mean I understand them. With a premonition, you can't force it to come. It chooses you. Sometimes a premonition is happenings that moment, sometimes in the future, sometimes it's sort of from the past. I don't yet know how to tell the difference. I wasn't sure if I'd ever know how to accurately understand the difference. I was probably going to have to trust Neilson and let him hook me up with people that knew more about my craziness than I did. Hell, if I was going to have to deal with this type of shit, I needed to be properly trained. I had no idea when this particular vision had happened.

Right on cue, Calvin said, "When did that happen? What we saw. Or has it happened?"

"I don't have any clue," I admitted. "I don't know how to tell either."

We lapsed into more silence. Much to both of our surprise, we heard a knock on the door. Calvin motioned me to move, and he drew his gun. As he crossed into the living room out of the kitchen, he disappeared from my view. When he reached the front door, I heard him say, "Who is it?"

"It's Annie and Neilson. Let us in bozo!" I heard Annie say.

Calvin sighed audibly and opened the front door. I walked into the living room to greet them. Annie looked at me and said, "You had me worried. I called you back, and you never answered. I was afraid you'd actually killed Calvin. Thought you might have been hiding the body or something," she joked.

Calvin looked at me. "You called Annie?" he asked. "Yeah, I told you as you were waking up. Remember? I sort of freaked out when you weren't coming to."

"Yeah, and Annie called me when you didn't answer. We thought we better-come check on you all," Neilson said.

I was suddenly acutely aware of how little clothing I was wearing in front of company. Neilson was nice enough to keep his eyes averted while I excused myself to go change. I went into the bedroom and grabbed a t-shirt and threw back on my sweatpants. I drug my feet as long as I could. I didn't want to go talk about my vision. I wanted to go to sleep. I wanted to forget what I'd seen. I wanted all this to be over and to never have to think about the gray skin and blank eyes again. I wanted my normal life back. But I couldn't do that. I couldn't have that. I walked back to the living room, and it became clear that Calvin had warned them about the coming news. He was waiting on me though. I didn't blame him. Where did I start?

Neilson seemed to sense my apprehension. I crossed the room and took a seat in the place he'd left beside him on the sofa. He looked at me and said, "Just start at the beginning. We need to know exactly what you saw. Has this type of thing happened to you before?"

"Yes, I've had tons of these visions, but none like this. Sometimes when I have one, it's a warning about something coming. Sometimes it's something that is happening right when I see it. Other times, it's something that's in the past, like something that has already happened. I haven't figured out how to tell the difference yet."

"That's okay," Neilson assured me. "Just start telling us what you saw."

Annie was weirdly quiet and tense. She seemed to be playing off of my emotions. I was so high-strung tonight that it was no wonder that she was tense as an empath.

"Well, I went to bed. I dreamed I was at the lodge at the hiking trail and lake. At first, I didn't know where I was."

"How did you figure it out?" Neilson asked.

"Well, the more that Gabe, you know the Gabe I mentioned before, moved around the lodge, I noticed familiar elements. I've been inside a few times over the years."

"Okay, so you recognized the space. Were you looking through his eyes?"

"Not at first. At first, I was situated in the middle of the room, fixed, and not able to move. Then I focused on his energy, and my perspective shifted to his view. I'm not sure how that happened."

"That's fine. It's not important right now. Go on."

"Well, when I was fixed, I could see the bloodstained carpet. I could see how nasty the space was. I heard him tell someone on the phone that he needed their help, that they needed to hurry before people got suspicious that the lodge was closed, he needed to clean the place up."

"Do you know who he was talking to?" Annie asked.

"I don't know. He mentioned they were cooperating because of the money. It sounded like he had bribed someone into helping or blackmailed them."

"Well, that's a classic sociopath trait," Annie added.

"Yeah, it is. Then he went across to the deep freeze that was in the kitchen area." My voice started to shake. Calvin stood and came over to put his hand on my shoulder.

"Take your time. It's okay," he said much more calmly than he felt.

"I'm okay. It's just when he opened the deep freeze there were body parts."

"Like other hands?" Neilson asked.

"Yes, but other parts too. There were legs. There were hands and arms. And there were heads. I recognized one for sure."

"Heads?" Neilson said looking quite grim.

"Yes. One of them was the nice landscaping man. I used to chat with him every single time I went out there. I didn't see him the day the hand was discovered. Now I figure it was because he was murdered already. He used the lodge as his little safe haven, and Gabe apparently wanted to use that space as his lair."

Suddenly Neilson and Annie seemed to understand why I was so disturbed. They too looked as bad as I felt. Well, they looked almost as bad as I felt. I felt pretty icky about then. The image of those glasslike open eyes was haunting me. I couldn't shake them out of my mind's eye.

Neilson looked at me. "You know I won't tell anyone that you gave us this lead. I won't put you in jeopardy, so don't worry about that. We will just say we needed to check it out for our investigation. I'll say it was a hunch I had. No one will know outside of this room that you had this vision."

"Thank you," I said shakily. "I want to help, but it does make me nervous to make him even madder. We have to find him before he kills Alice. Oh God, I hope she's still alive."

"We'll find her. We'll find him, and when we do, we'll shoot first and ask questions later. That son of a bitch is going to get what he has coming. He won't get away with this."

Chapter 20

The next couple of hours were extremely long. We sat in the living room, going over and over every single detail of my vision. Eventually, I got frustrated and grabbed Neilson's arm. When I touched him, I was able to let him access my energy so that he could see the way I'd let Calvin see. He was also so disturbed he had to excuse himself for a moment. Turns out he also knew the landscaper. He attended a book club with him, and it ripped him up to see him like that.

On the other hand, Annie held her shit together like a freaking champ when I showed her. She had a harsh look on her face. She hardened and became extremely protective of my involvement in the case. I was beginning to wonder if I reminded her of her sister. It's the same way Kate had always treated me, like a sister.

Calvin and Neilson excused themselves to the kitchen to talk in private, but Annie stayed with me. She was worried about leaving me alone. She asked me about other times I'd had visions. I told her the only other time I'd had a vision this bad was when Kate died. I told her that I had laid down for a nap and dreamed that she was killed. When I got up, I called her phone over and over. Eventually, her friend had answered and told me what had happened. That's when I realized I had watched her die. I'd seen it through the eyes of her killer. I'd felt what he felt. I'd heard what he heard. I'd seen what he'd seen.

She looked at me so sadly. She could tell I was rattled. I didn't want to sit around and do nothing, but I wasn't ready to do what was necessary to get this guy. The biggest puzzle for me was that I didn't know why I couldn't properly sense this guy's energy to tell if he was good or bad. Well, let me rephrase this. I knew now, but I didn't understand why I couldn't tell previous to this vision.

I asked her, "Do you know of anyone that can mind map?"

"No, it's almost unheard of," she said.

"Well, I can do it. I can't sense Gabe's energy very well though. I keep trying, but..."

"Stop trying. He might sense you goddamnit. Don't be an idiot!" Annie interrupted with true anger in her voice. "Don't make yourself a bigger target!"

"Oh, I'd never considered that."

There was silence between us for a moment or two.

"You can map?" she said with envy in her voice.

"Yeah, I did it for the first time the other day. I don't know how to do it well yet. Neilson was the one that told me what I had done."

"Oh my God. That's crazy!" she said. "I wish I could map. I'd quit my job and start a consulting business. I could do so much good with that ability. I'm a boring psychic. I want some cool ability like that. Mine are very run of the mill."

"I don't know. It's not all it's cracked up to be. It seems to be getting me into a lot of trouble. I wish we could swap," I joked.

"Well, I wish we could swap too," she laughed.

At that moment, Neilson and Calvin came back into the room. They both looked tired. The thing about the last few days is that none of us had been getting any sleep. None of us were mentally rested. None of us knew when we'd be able to forget the picture of all those dead body parts in clear grocery sacks in the freezer of that lodge. It wasn't likely something we'd forget overnight.

Neilson said, "Look, we need to go to the station and figure out where to go from here. Are you comfortable coming in with us? Remember that I won't tell anyone that the information came from you. We will come up with a story."

"Yeah, let's go," I said, getting up from the couch.

Everyone looked at me with a weird look as I jumped back suddenly from the middle of the room. I gasped loudly.

Chapter 21

Ghost man was back to talk. I know I've told you this before, but I'm going to say it again. I fucking hate ghosts. They are nasty little things that are overly aggressive and damn downright mean. This ghost was pretty pissed off because he had lost me for a few days, so he'd had no one to talk to. Well, unless he'd found the man from the liquor store. He was glaring at me like I was the one to kill him instead of...well I assumed instead of Gabe, but hell if I knew for sure.

"Lady, where the hell have you been? I've been looking for you, but you never come home."

"Uh, yeah, that's a little complicated," I said. Calvin and Neilson were looking around to see who I was talking to, but Annie was squinting into the middle of the room like she was looking for a gnat that was flying around near her drink. Obviously, they couldn't see ghosts. I was the only one stuck dealing with this.

"Well, Lady, you have to help me. I can't keep hanging around here. It's so frustrating. It's also getting pretty lonely."

"I don't know how to help you. I'm sorry. You don't believe in God, so that isn't going to bring you any peace. What do you want to do?" I said in a very snarky tone.

Okay, I know. I was being a real bitch, but this guy was getting on my last nerve. I guess I should have felt empathetic for him, but he called me lady over and over. It was the sneer in his voice. I bet he was the type of person who snapped at waitresses and didn't leave a tip if he had to wait even a couple minutes longer than he wanted.

"I want to go somewhere else. If you can see me, you have to help me. That's got to be a rule somewhere."

Calvin said, "Who are you talking to?"

"I believe I'm talking to Wilson's brother. He wants help moving on. He's also being a massive pain in my ass," I said.

"Hey now, I just want your help. You're the one being a bitch and refusing to help me," he said.

"Now you better shut up. If you call me a bitch again, I'm going to do my best to make sure you never move on," I threatened.

Neilson looked both nervous and humored. "Tell him I said we are trying to find his body. Maybe that will help put him at ease."

"Does he not know that I can hear him?" ghost man said.

"He can hear you," I said with a little humor.

"Look, Mike, I know that you aren't happy that you're dead. I'm not happy you won't leave me alone, but I don't know how to help you."

"Well, you better figure it out."

"Threatening me doesn't really help me like you more, you know that, right?"

Calvin was looking hard at the television screen. I think he thought he was looking in the right direction, but he was really looking several feet to the left, so he just looked really silly to Mike and to me.

"What the fuck is he looking at? Does he think he will see me in the reflection of the TV?"

I chose to ignore that snarky comment because I kind of agreed.

"Do you know who killed you?"

"Nope. I don't know his name. I need you to find him, and I want you to cut him apart. That motherfucker was going to throw my body parts in the lake, but you interrupted him, so he made a beeline out of the way and dropped my hand. I have figured that much out. It appears to be more than you have figured out."

Well, he was really making me mad now. "We are working quite hard. We have a few more barriers to cross than you do as a flippin' dead guy. We have rules. We have red tape."

"Whatever. You guys are just like my brother. All about the rules and all about what he could and couldn't do for me."

So, here's the reason he can't move on. He blamed his brother for his death. He didn't have to say it. I could sense it. He was furious that his brother hadn't started really looking for him. He was also deeply hurt. He wanted to feel missed, and right now, all he felt was alone. I felt myself softening to him.

"Your brother is worried about you. I can't tell him you're dead. He wouldn't believe me, but he's been digging to find out why you haven't contacted him yet. He really does care," I tried to assure him.

He just glared back at me. "Well, he has a really funny way of showing it. I bet he'd have let me die if he'd known ahead of time. He doesn't love me. I'm the one that's been in and out of rehab. I'm the disgrace. He didn't even want people to know I was his twin brother. He just wanted to..."

Poof. He was gone. I didn't know if I should feel bad or relieved.

I said, "He's gone. He got too pissed off and poofed." They all just looked at me. "Oh, ghosts poof away if they get too angry, but he will be back."

"Did you learn anything new?"

"Yeah, Wilson's brother is a real asshole, but he's sad that Wilson doesn't appear to be looking too hard for him. He wants us to find his killer and decapitate him. He's a really lovely man," I said.

Neilson laughed. "Well, Wilson had been drug through the mud by his brother, but he probably should act like he cares more than he has been, but Wilson, he's just like that."

"Well, tell it to his dead twin brother. I think they are both assholes," I said.

Chapter 22

We all got our stuff and headed back to the station. They wanted to be extra careful with me, so they sent me in the car with Neilson. I guess they thought he was the most capable of getting me there safely. I wanted to ride with Calvin, but I was told, quite firmly I might add, no. It didn't really do any good to argue, so I decided to play nicely and cooperate. We were all under a lot of stress.

It was early, early morning, and all I wanted was a donut. I know, I'd eaten a crapload of food not long ago, but I was stressed. I wanted a freaking donut with jelly in the middle. As we drove away from my house, I turned to Neilson and asked if he would stop at the donut shop. At first, he thought I was making a cop joke, and he glared at me. Then he realized I was serious, and boy did he get excited. He told me the donuts were on him and headed straight to the best locally owned donut shop in town.

Everyone loves Luke's. He makes the donuts fresh every single morning. He has Bismarks. He has jelly filled. He has cake. He has every type of donut you could imagine. And boy oh boy, he makes one heck of a cinnamon roll.

Today, I wanted to get some good old lemon-filled glazed donuts. Neilson ordered two dozen. Apparently, he could eat a dozen himself, and he wanted me to have plenty. I mean, I was just really wanting a couple, but a girl won't complain about too many lemon-filled donuts when she's stressed out.

The good news was that Annie liked lemon filled donuts too, and she was in need of a pick me up. She had barely any sleep, and I was pretty sure she was coming down with a cold. I saw her drink straight from the cough syrup bottle before she joined Calvin, Neilson, and me in the conference room. She pulled up a chair and helped herself to the box of donuts I shoved to her.

Calvin, on the other hand, didn't appear to be hungry. He kept staring at me. I think he was waiting for me to have a breakdown, but I was holding it together. You see, I don't have time to freak out at the moment on things. I like to keep my life together until everything is over. I'd be in a real bind then though. I bet I'd need to sleep for a full week the way I've been feeling.

As we got settled in, Neilson said, "Look, we are going to put together a task force. We want you present, but we need to come up with a reason you are here."

"Okay," I said. "What do you think we should say if people ask?"

Calvin interjected, "I think we should say that you are still profiling and that you have a history of consulting on cases. Even if they don't believe it, it will keep you safe."

"I agree," Neilson said. "Keeping it simple is the least likely way to draw attention to the situation. The less attention was drawn, the less risk to be managed. Good plan, Stormy."

"Who are we including?" Annie asked. "I assume you will let me take part."

"Of course," said Neilson. "You have been invaluable, and you and Reba get along really well. We need you, Annie."

It's weird. I noticed that Neilson always called Annie by her first name, but he always called Calvin by his last name. The more I looked at Annie and at Neilson, I realized there was a vague resemblance between them. I suddenly wondered if they could be related. It did seem like a possibility. I didn't think there were father and daughter, but maybe they were niece and uncle or something.

"How are you related?" I blurted out.

They both looked at me in surprise. "He's my uncle," Annie said. "How did you know?"

"It's in the energy and in the looks. I just noticed. Sorry," I said apologetically.

Clearly, Calvin hadn't known. He looked a little taken aback, but not angry. Neilson also looked surprised that I could tell from the energy.

"What do you mean it's in the energy?" he asked me.

"Oh, I can see blood relative connections in energy. Is that unusual?" I asked, suddenly feeling self-conscious. Why is it always me with weird abilities?

"Everything about you is unusual," Neilson joked.

I grimaced. Well, I'd heard that one before, and it smarted a little. I could tell that Neilson meant nothing rude by it, but I was still a little perturbed. He seemed to pick up on it, and said, "Hey, I'm just kidding. I forget you aren't used to talking about your abilities, and that you are so reluctant to let people know. I was just kidding. Sorry if I offended you."

"It's fine," I said as casually as I could.

Okay, so no one in their right mind would think anything was fine if they heard the way I just said that.

Chapter 23

Now before I continue, I think it's worth noting that I'm not an unreasonable person. I wasn't mad at Neilson; I was more a little huffy. It's just, I've been made fun of many times in my life if someone suspected I was different. I don't like to make my differences stand out too much. I learned that it's like survival of the fittest. If you show weakness or non-homogeneity, people jump on that like flies on honey.

The room was rather quiet and stiff while Neilson and I sized each other up. I guess he realized that I did not want to talk more about it, so he moved on.

"So, as we gather people, they will be heading in here. We need to pick the right group of folks so that we can properly catch this bastard. I will not be choosing anyone that does not have ability, because I think it will be hard to work with those that only have half the information."

Oh brother. Here we go. He said that no one would have to know about my vision, and he was already waffling on that note. "I thought you weren't going to tell anyone about my vision," I said stiffly.

"Well, I'm not going to tell just anyone. I thought you might be okay if everyone had ability. I will only select my most trusted people."

Calvin chimed in, "I don't like that plan."

"Yeah, I don't either," said Annie.

"Well, I didn't ask you two," snapped Neilson. "I asked Reba."

"Well, I don't like it either, but it might be necessary," I added grudgingly. "I guess it's all right."

Calvin nor Annie looked like they approved of my concession at all, but Neilson seemed pretty damn pleased.

"Remember that I cooperated if I decide later to tell you to stick something up your ass," I snapped. "Since you already have me where you want me, I noticed you backed out of your earlier promise. It took a solid five minutes at that."

Neilson had the decency to look embarrassed, as he should. He averted his gaze away from mine.

"Well, what are you waiting for? Start rounding people up," I growled. Okay, I admit it. I'm getting a little cranky. I've had almost no sleep, and now I felt like I was getting drug into one hell of a deep mess.

My annoyance was enough to shove Neilson out of his chair. He hurried from the room. Calvin and Annie looked at me.

"You know you don't have to do this," Annie said. "You could tell him no. I love him, and he's a good person, but he can be a real ass."

"Yeah, well, I mean, what other choice do we have?"

"You could leave. He can't make you stay," Calvin added. "I'd have your back, I promise."

I was touched. I knew he meant it. He would put his job on the line to keep me safe. Something about that really made me even more attracted to him. What the hell? Was I lusting after him right now? It hardly seemed like the appropriate time to be thinking about sex.

I smiled at him. "It will all be okay. Let's just get this done. I don't want to keep waffling around and making no progress. I want this guy caught so I can go home and not worry anymore."

***

Over the next few minutes, a random assortment of people came in and joined us. They all seemed a little confused at why they were being sent to the conference room. What's worse is that those who weren't being sent to the conference room seemed downright hostile. I think they thought that it was some privilege to be sent in here. Funny thing is, all I wanted was to leave.

Within half an hour, there were five other people in the room. Three male cops by the names of Scott, Nick, and Seal, and two female cops by the names of Sara and Leslie. They all seemed nice enough, but man oh man were they curious about me. I felt like I was the key suspect in a murder case the way there were interrogating me. It was not making Annie and Calvin very happy either. They clearly thought they all needed to mind their own business.

When Neilson joined the room, he took a seat at the head of the table. He waited for the room to quiet down, and then he looked at me. What did he think I was going to do? I wasn't taking point.

He clearly got the picture that I wasn't talking, so he started in. "I guess you all are curious why I've called you in here today." There were a lot of head nods at that comment.

"We have a very serious case that we've gathered some information on. I want to read you all in because I plan on you being part of this task force. Miss Parker is here to consult on this case because she has some very valuable expertise in this area. Well, that, and she is involved with this case."

Heads swiveled my direction briefly, but everyone turned their attention back to Neilson immediately. "The case of the hand and the missing pregnant woman, yeah, well they are connected. Alice was Miss Parker's client, as some of you may know. Alice was abducted because the man who cut off the hand was following Reba. We have reason to believe that he has killed at least two people, and he is still on the move. We need to catch him fast."

The room was so quiet you could have heard a stomach growl. I didn't really get the feeling that these people wanted to be part of this investigation any more than I did. On the upside for them, their happy asses got paid to put their lives in jeopardy. I did not.

"As you all may have noticed, there is no one in this room that does not have some sort of a rather special skill set. Miss Parker has quite a few skills as well," he continued. "She has had a vision of the location of at least two bodies and a hell of a lot of evidence. We also have the name of the suspect. His name is Gabe."

The room was utterly silent. "Now, as we move forward, I want to give you all the opportunity to ask me some questions. What questions do you have?"

Sara was the first to speak. "I mean, do we have to be part of this?" she asked.

Neilson looked shrewd, and so did Calvin and Annie. "Yes. It's not optional," he added curtly.

Seal spoke next. "Do we know who the victims are yet?"

"Well, actually I do," I said. "One victim is the landscaper from the hiking trail and lake, and the other is Wilson's twin brother." The room went to buzzing with whispers. Well, that was the end of the questions.

Chapter 24

Neilson clearly disapproved of me telling them that, but what the hell? Didn't he think they didn't deserve to know ahead of time? Apparently not, because he gave me quite the filthy look. Well, he could shove it where the Sun doesn't shine. I thought they had the right to know.

"Quiet down, quiet down," he said. "We do believe that this is the correct answer, but not a word of this can be spoke outside of this room. Are we perfectly clear on the confidential nature of this case?"

Everyone muttered, "Yes."

"Good, because I know every person that has this information, and if any of it leaks, I promise you that you will find yourself unemployed so fast you won't even have time to hiccup."

More crickets. He could play hardball when he needed, which I decided was probably a good thing considering what we were up against.

Over the next couple of hours, they were all filled in on every single detail of the case. They learned about the ghost visits. They learned about the SUV. They heard about it all. It was exhausting. They realized that they were going to need to be discreet as to not draw unwanted attention to the case.

As late morning approached, Neilson realized that Alice's husband hadn't been by today. I too had noticed this. I'd been watching and waiting for him to show up.

Neilson went into the squad room and asked to make sure we hadn't missed it. No cigar. When he came back in, he asked for two volunteers to go and do a well check on her husband.

"I'll go," Nick said.

"Me too," said Scott.

"Great. I need you to call me before you approach the door. I also need you to call me as soon as you get back in the car. I want you to make sure he is all right, but I also want you to check him out for unusual behavior. We can never be too careful when dealing with a case like this. Make sure he hasn't heard anything about a ransom or something, and that he doesn't feel like he's putting her in danger by talking to the police."

"Sure, Boss. We got it covered," said Nick.

The left the room and headed out. The rest of us had been given tasks to do, and we all broke out into what needed to be done. Neilson and I were the only ones left in the conference room. He looked at me. "Are you still pissed off at me?" he asked.

I laughed. "A little, but not too bad. I get that you have a lot on your plate. It isn't easy managing a case like this. I just want you to be more forthright with me. I hate the way that you say one thing and do another."

"Well, I'm sorry I put you in a weird spot. I shouldn't have done that. It's just, this case, it's not something to mess around with."

"I know."

"Well, I'll let you work. I'll update everyone when I know more," and he left the room.

***

A little while later, Neilson started gathering the troops. As we all got settled, we noted his grim expression. This really didn't bode well at all. Scott and Nick walked into the squad room, and they headed directly back to the conference room. That couldn't be a good sign, either. Well frickety-frack. They must not have found him, or he was dead.

After Nick and Scott joined us, Neilson said, "We have a rather large problem to deal with. Alice's husband,

Anthony, he's missing. All the furniture is there, but there is a mailbox full of mail, two newspapers on the lawn, and no car in the driveway. He also didn't answer the door. We are working on a search warrant right now. Hopefully, we get that by the end of the day."

"Could he have just left town for a day or two?" asked Annie.

"Doubtful," said Nick. "The neighbors said they haven't seen him in a couple days. One of them said he looked really pale when they saw him last, and he asked if they would look after the dog for him. He said he was worried that something bad was going to happen to him. Also, he was told to stay in town and lay low for a few days by us, or should I say, by Neilson."

"Well, that's awful," I said. "We need to look for him. What are we going to do?" I felt the panic rising in my throat. My stomach clenched. Was he already dead? What if he was added to the collection of limbs in that deep freeze by now?

Neilson shot me a warning look. We're on it. I promise, he thought while making eye contact with me. At least it looked like he too realized what a bad sign it was that no one could find Anthony. Neilson looked at me and said, "I think I have a job for you while we wait."

Chapter 25

Neilson wanted me to work with a sketch artist. I didn't object to that at all. If we had a rendering of this guy, Gabe, then we could use it. If we didn't, there really wasn't a way to explain how we knew it was him. I was going to say that this was the sketch of the man following me. While I felt a little weird lying, it helped a lot that I was told to lie by a cop. At least I wasn't going to go to jail for this.

He led me to a little private room. I sat in there alone for a few minutes before a woman entered the room. She was tall, African American, and had a warm smile. She was wearing a bright orange dress with black sandals. She appeared to be around thirty if I had to guess. She said, "Hey, there! Are you Reba?"

"I sure am," I said.

"Great, I'm the sketch artist. My name is Courtney. Have you ever done this before?"

"No, I haven't. I'm a little nervous," I admitted.

"Pish-posh. No need to be worried. We will get through this together. I'm actually a local artist, but I freelance with the department when they need me."

"Oh, that's cool. I'm a local photographer, so you could say we are in sister disciplines."

"Ohhhh....that's awesome. I bet you already have an eye for detail. This should make my job so much easier."

Her voice was a little singsong for someone working a case like this, but then I realized she probably didn't know many of the details at all. She was just here to draw a picture and get paid.

I watched her as she set out her materials. I was surprised to see that she brought colored pencils as well. She had a big drawing pad, and she sat down at the table.

"I prefer to not use the easel, but if this bothers you, I can set it up. Some people don't like to see while I'm drawing."

"No, no, I'm fine seeing," I assured her.

She said, "Great! Let's get started. I want you to start with vague descriptions. I mean, tell me the face shape and hair type. Then, we will go from there."

"Okay, his face is rather round, and he has a buzz cut. His hair is dark brown or black."

"Great," she said as she rapidly sketched. "Like this?"

I looked at the shape of the face. It seemed close. "Yes, I think."

"That's fine. We can always try again if it's not quite right. We can use the first sketch as a base."

"Awesome. That makes me feel better."

"Now, I don't add color until the end."

"Sure, that makes sense."

"Now, let's talk about the eyes."

"His eyes are rather far set apart. Dark brown, I think, but he has big eyes with long eyelashes."

"Good!" she encouraged. "What about this?"

"No, a little closer together than that."

"Okay." She continued to sketch and erase. After a few moments, she asked, "Is this closer?"

"Oh yeah, that's perfect!"

"Awesome Sauce!" she said brightly! Man did I wish I had her carefree attitude today.

"What next?" I asked.

"Let's talk about the nose."

"His nose is average size on the bottom, but it's rather slim at the top." I was focusing as hard as I could on his face. Luckily, I have a photographic memory, so it seemed to be working pretty well. "I think the end is a bit smooshed and pointed down."

"Awesome, I was fixing to ask you about the tip. What about his eyebrows? Thick, thin?"

"Oh God, his eyebrows are super thick. And he almost has a unibrow."

"Okay, that's good. Give me a few minutes." She was sketching at top speed. I couldn't imagine how she was able to do this. She was so good. It was almost like she was pulling it out of my head. Oh my God, she was pulling it out of my head. I could feel her energy against mine. I said nothing about it, though.

"Now the lips," she said. "How big are they?"

"They are quite slim, but then his cheekbones are quite round."

"Great. Got it," she said happily.

This went on for a while, but eventually, we moved over to color. It took her about half an hour to add the color, but then we called Neilson in. He looked at the sketch, and I could tell he was impressed. It looked exactly like the Gabe from my vision. He told me to wait here, and he would be back shortly. He escorted Courtney out, and then he returned.

"Well, that went quite well. Did it take more than one try?"

"Nope. Did you know she has ability?"

"Yes, I do. She has never spoke with me about it, but I know she has it. I can sense how strong it is. I take it you could tell, too?"

"Yes. She has a lot of ability, but she never mentioned it."

"Well, she is the best sketch artist I've ever found, but now is not the time to talk about that. Calvin and I are going to go to the lodge in a little while, but we just got the warrant for Anthony's house. Come join us in the conference room. We need to talk, and the others are already there."

Chapter 26

The type of paralyzing fear that clenched my throat muscles when he said that he and Calvin were going to the lodge isn't at all similar to the kind I'd experienced before. This time it was full on panic, raspy breath, and utter disorientation. I didn't want them to go. I didn't want Calvin to go. Now that I thought about it, I was sure that dead-on-the-floor Calvin had been at the lodge. I couldn't let him go. I had to prevent it.

Before I could even object, Neilson turned to walk out of the room. I hollered, "Hey, wait!" but he didn't even turn around and look at me. It's like he just didn't want to deal with me. Maybe that asshole was a bad guy after all. Well, well, well, that stopped him in his tracks.

"Would you quit that! I don't know what that flash meant, but I'm certainly not going to kill Calvin. You need to get the fuck ahold of yourself."

Well, well, well. Look who was being an asshole again. I stared at him hard. "I don't appreciate your tone. You have the training to deal with this type of stuff. I just got drug into the middle of it."

He looked embarrassed again. I could tell the stress was getting to him. I get it. I know he's just human, but I still thought he needed to be more professional. "Also, don't bitch about what you hear me think. I shouldn't have to control my thoughts," I growled. I slapped my wall all the way up.

"Look, I'm sorry. I'm just a little stressed out."

"You know, I really don't give a shit," I said as I stormed by him.

I went straight to the conference room. You see, people have never really liked to be around me when I'm angry. People want to describe my anger as suffocating. My mom always said my anger sucks the air out of the room. I think it's because I'm a high-level empath, and I project my anger out of my energy. Needless to say, everyone turned and looked at me as I entered the room.

Silence. Annie's eyebrows almost disappeared into her hair. She knew what was up. She sensed my utter fury, but she just didn't know why. Calvin reached to put his hand on my arm as I collapsed into the chair. He immediately yanked it back and sucked in his breath. I was running hot.

I've learned not to touch people when I'm upset or angry because they get shocked. I'm not talking in metaphors either. I'm saying I shoot electricity at people, and they howl in pain. Calvin took it like a champ though. He was staring me with wide eyes when Neilson walked in.

Neilson stopped right beside me. He looked down at me. "Do you always stomp off when you're pissed off? Or do I get special treatment?" he asked.

"I try not to accidentally electrocute people, so I walk off. I wouldn't touch me right now."

"Noted," he said.

He crossed to the head of the table before turning to the group at large. They were all observing our go-between with interest. I got the feeling people didn't really stand up to Neilson often. When someone did, it looked like he stomped them into submission. I think the others were just impressed by my guts.

Neilson cleared his throat, and all eyes shifted to him. "We've got our search warrant for Anthony and Alice's house. We need to start there. Afterward, Calvin and I are going to the lodge to see what we find. I need the rest of you to be ready to jump into action immediately if needed. Annie, you are on Reba. Calvin, you're with me. Leslie and Scott, I want you backing us up. Seal, Nick, Sara, I want you patrolling. I will give you details shortly. Are we clear?"

"Uh, no. What do you want me to do?" I asked.

"I want you to go back to the safe house, and I want you to lay low. You don't have the training to deal with this situation."

"I can help. Just tell me what to do."

"You can take an order."

"You forget I'm not working for you," I snapped.

He sighed. "Would you please cooperate? You have already done a ton. You will just be distracting us if we think he's trying to get to you."

"Finnnne."

Annie said, "We will do something fun! It'll be great."

Clearly, she was trying to diffuse my anger. "Yeah, sure," I said.

Neilson turned to Calvin. "Are you ready to go to Anthony's house?"

"Yep," Calvin replied.

Everyone stood, ready to jump into action. I followed Calvin out of the room and pulled him down a nearby hallway. "Promise me you will be careful," I whispered.

We were standing close and out of sight of the others. He stepped closer to me, laced his fingers in my hair, and leaned down to kiss me. Every fiber of my being lit on fire. It was like his touch turned me into a human torch. He deepened his kiss and pulled me against him. We heard a snicker and broke apart. It was Courtney.

"Sorry. I forgot my colored pencils," she said.

"No problem," we said in unison.

As she passed by us, Calvin locked my gaze. "I promise."

Chapter 27

I was all nerves and knotted stomached as I waited for them to leave and search the house. Before Calvin left, he gave me a reassuring squeeze. Annie and I had decided we were staying until we heard about how it went. Then, we were going to get Ozzie and go to the safe house. I told her I was sorry she was missing out, and she laughed at me. I guess she didn't mind being my babysitter.

We sat at her desk, chatting. Wilson walked by and stopped. "What are you two little ladies doing?" he said in a very condescending way. "Talking about getting your nails done?"

I can't imagine why his dead brother would hate him. "No, we are talking about murder," Annie said.
That shut him the hell up. He walked away, muttering under his breath.

"Is he always like that?" I asked.

"Yep. He's a misogynistic jerk. He treats every woman like shit."

"Yeah, he doesn't seem like the good type."

"Is there a good type of man?"

"Well, I like to think so."

"You are still holding out for Stormy then?"

"I'm not holding out for anything. It's been forever since I've been in a relationship. They always end the same...badly."

"I have to admit, he doesn't seem too bad. He does seem to like you a lot."

"I don't know. I guess we will just have to wait and see. Can I tell you something?"

"Of course," she said.

"Well, I had a vision of Neilson standing over Calvin with a gun. I know you're related, but like what else could that mean?"

"You mean, Calvin was dead?"

"It sure looked like it. There was a lot of blood, and he was on the ground."

"Shit. I don't know. Do you know where it happened?"

"I think at the lodge."

"Well, you have to tell them."

"They know, and Neilson is pissed that I keep second guessing him."

"Oh, that's why," she said.

Then her phone rang. It was Neilson. He told her the house was empty. It looked like Anthony had left in a rush. He told her they were going straight to the lodge.

I felt my stomach tighten. They shouldn't be doing that. They didn't need to rush it. I could feel every instinct telling me they were making the wrong decision, but it was out of my hands. I just had to wait.

Annie sensed my dread, so she suggested we headed to get Ozzie. I reluctantly agreed. As we gathered up our things, I thought about Calvin being shot. Suddenly, I got the light and airy feeling. Oh shit.

Annie must have sensed it too. She asked me, "What just happened?"

"Sometimes my gut tells me things. I thought about Calvin getting shot, and my gut told me it was right."

"Do you get a light and airy feeling?"

"Yes."

"I get that too. Well, I'm not sure what we can do but hope and wait."

***

A little while later, we pulled up in my mom's driveway. We got out and knocked on her front door. There was no answer. I felt fear dripping down me again. I knocked louder. Annie drew her gun, and she tried the knob. It was unlocked.

Annie motioned for me to go back to the car. I shook my head no and walked straight through the door. The living room was empty. No mom. No Ozzie. I could hear running water coming from the back of the house. Annie and I moved that way. I called out, "Mom?"

No response. I yanked open her bedroom door. The master bathroom door was closed. I walked over and opened it.

There she was. Leaned over the side of the bathtub giving Ozzie a bath. "Oh, Lord have mercy. I didn't hear you, love," my mom said.

I burst into tears. I'd been convinced she was hurt or worse. My reaction scared her. "Honey, what's wrong?"

"I've just been stressed. I'm okay," I replied. Annie was standing there, awkwardly. I remembered my manners and introduced her. "Mom, this is Annie. Annie, this is my mom, Rebecca."

"Nice to meet you," my mom said.

"Likewise. I've heard so much about you," Annie said brightly.

Ozzie was dripping with soap, but I noticed he didn't look too good. "Mom, what's wrong with Oz?"

"He's thrown up a couple times. That's why I'm bathing him. I ran out of dog food, so I went and bought a little bag. I don't think it agreed with him very well."

"Oh no! I might need to take him to vet to get checked out." I saw Ozzie's tail droop.

"No, Mom. I'm fine," he said. I ignored him. Mom got him out of the tub, and Annie and I took him to the living room. After a bath, Ozzie runs zoomies. Zoomies are when he runs laps around the house. He just laid there though. Yep, he needed a vet visit for sure. When he isn't up and running around after a bath, it always means he isn't feeling well.

You see, Ozzie hates going to vet. No matter how nice they are to him, he squeals like he dying. He cries and makes such a fuss. It's actually a little embarrassing for me, but not as bad as when a big old Rottweiler does it. At least my dog is little.

I picked up my cell phone as my mom offered us each a cup of tea. I nodded, and Annie offered to help her. They walked out of the room together.

I rung the vet. They agreed that I should bring him in. They said they had an opening in an hour if I could make it. I went and joined my mom and Annie in the kitchen. I could tell Annie had filled her in because my mom looked worried.

"Annie, I wasn't going to worry her."

"She's your mom and one of your best friends. She had the right to know. Plus, now she will be extra careful!"

I saw my mom beaming. She loved Annie as much as I did. It was hard not to. She was one of those sincere and caring people that you were just drawn to. I'd always suspected my mom had ability, but she never spoke of it. I suspect she was scared people would think she was crazy. When I told her about what happened at the cafeteria in school, she had told me to never let people make me feel like being different was bad, but that sometimes it's best not to advertise our differences to people because sometimes it's hard to know who you can trust. That's stuck with me all these years.

I told them that Ozzie had a vet appointment in an hour, and my mom offered to take him. I wouldn't let her though. I wanted to be there to take care of him. I don't have any children, so Ozzie is my kid.

We drank our tea and chatted for a while. I was growing increasingly nervous. As the appointment time neared, we left my mom's house with a promise to call her and update her later. Ozzie was thrilled to be coming with us, but he was still moping around as we got in the car.

Chapter 28

As I directed Annie to the vet I use on the outskirts of town, my stomach started getting nauseous. I felt like I couldn't breathe properly. Ozzie picked up on this too, so he got super fussy. For him, it was probably a combination of me being anxious and him being scared of the vet. He knew when we went this way, it was always a vet trip. He was busy yowling and begging me not to take him. Annie could hear him through me, and she was getting quite a kick out of the whole situation.

Little Ozzie was not. You see, he is very sensitive to my emotions, my health, and my safety. He self-trained himself to notice these things, so I knew my anxiety was throwing him off even worse. I tried to take deep calming breaths and ignore that gnawing worry in my belly, but it wasn't working very well.

We pulled up outside of Lisa's Veterinarian Clinic, suddenly I felt like the car was spinning around me. Luckily, Annie had been driving. I couldn't tell if something was wrong or if I was having a panic attack. Were they already at the lodge? Was Calvin dead? Oh, God. I couldn't think about any of that. Annie was observing me carefully.

"You know, I don't always like Neilson, but he's not a murderer. It's all going to be okay. He loves Calvin like a son. Calvin saved Neilson's ass when he was just a rookie on the team. Neilson had him riding along with him, and he stopped someone. That guy pulled a gun and shot Neilson. Calvin took down the perp and got Neilson medical assistance. It was week one for Calvin. Since then, Neilson told me he will always value Calvin."

I knew she was just trying to help, but nothing she said was going to make me feel any better. Something was going to go wrong. I just knew it. My gut told me so, and my gut is always right. I managed a weak smile at her and got out of the car. I picked Ozzie up and took him inside. Annie came with me.

As we entered the front door, a commotion ensued. Apparently, the massive German Shepard that was standing on the scale was scared of other dogs. He saw Ozzie and took the hell off. He ran right into me and knocked me sideways. Annie grabbed Ozzie as we hit the ground. The owner of the German Shepard ran after him. I was busy fussing over Ozzie. Poor baby smacked the ground hard. He seemed no worse for wear though. The vet tech was so apologetic to me, but I shushed her concerns away. We got little Ozzie checked in, and he started whimpering really loud, so they took us in the back.

When we got back there, Ozzie started gagging. He was gagging and gagging. I was getting really scared when he threw up what looked like a shoelace. Turns out, it might not have been the food that upset the little guy's stomach. It was probably my sneaker from the other day. The vet came hurrying in. She said they needed to run some tests to make sure he didn't have an obstruction of some sort. She poked all around on him, and he howled like he was dying, but that was nothing compared to when they stuck the thermometer up his bottom.

I think the vet could understand him because she was grinning really big. He was screaming about "my ass, my ass." I could have died with laughter, but I held it together. She left me in the room with Annie, and she and the vet tech took him to do some x-rays.

Well, let me tell you, I could hear him screaming all the way down the hall. He was a crying and a begging me to take him home. He said, "I will never eat another shoe. Just don't leave me here all alone." So yeah, he was milking as much sympathy as he could out of them back there. After a few minutes, they came back in.

The vet said, "Well, he should be able to pass what's left, but I'd like to keep him overnight to make sure he's okay. We can give him some medicine that will help. He should be feeling much better by tomorrow."

"Don't leave me here!" he begged. "Please! I'll be a good boy, Mama!"

I sighed loudly. "You think he really needs to stay?" I asked.

"Yes, I want to make sure it passes with ease. If he's here, we could handle any complications easier than if we let him go home."

"Okay, is someone here all night?"

"Yes, Ma'am. He will be in good hands."

"Okay, I said reluctantly. He gets scared in small crates. Can you put him in a big one?"

"We sure can."

"Then, I guess he can stay." I scooped him up and started loving him. His tail was all droopy, and I could tell he was really mad at me. He wouldn't even look at me. Freakin' A. I felt so bad.

I handed him over to the vet tech with a promise to see him tomorrow. As we went back to the front, I paid and left my number and my mom's number as emergency contacts. Then, Annie and I went outside into the warm air and got back in the car.

Chapter 29

We were quiet as we drove back towards the safe house. My mind was racing, but Annie is always the best. She seemed to notice that I needed some time to think. One of my favorite things about Annie is that she respects silence. She allows silence to be comfortable, and so we drove on in pure blissfulness.

    Okay, maybe not exactly. I was stressed out. Ozzie was still trying to talk to me from the vet. I can hear him from pretty far away, so needless to say, I was sad. He was begging me to come back, and I kept telling him it would be okay. I couldn't wait till we were out of range. He was breaking my heart. As his voice dwindled, I felt relieved, but also frustrated. I'd never left him at the vet overnight. I could sense his fear like he could hear the crinkle of chips from the other end of the house. I hoped he knew I was just trying to keep him safe.

Safe. My stomach knotted up. Calvin's face popped into my mind. Something was seriously wrong. I couldn't tell what though, but if my gut said so, it was so. It was 100% accurate.

I thought as we sat at a stoplight. All of a sudden, I could feel Calvin's energy. It brushed up against mine like he was standing right beside me. My map popped up spontaneously, and Calvin was in grave danger. Red surrounding his energy, and then black—the color that meant death.

Then, I wasn't in the car anymore. I was back in the lodge, surrounded by blood and people. Gabe was there. He was fleeing out the door as Neilson leveled his gun to shoot. At the same time, Calvin lunged to grab Gabe. Neilson's gun fired. Calvin went down hard. Blood was pooling around him on the ground, and he was gasping for air. Neilson was running towards Gabe, towards Calvin. He stopped right over Calvin and looked down at him, gun still extended, clearly deciding not to run after Gabe. Neilson dropped to his knees as the others came running in.

"Man down, man down!" Neilson yelled into his walkie. "Get us help. We have a fucking man down!"

***

Then I was back in the car, and I was sobbing. I don't actually know how long my vision took. Annie was parked on the side of the road. I also didn't know exactly where we were either. It looked like she had tried to take a shortcut, but she'd ran into construction and had been routed around. There was a big warehouse I could see.

"What did you see?" she demanded. "Please tell me."

"Calvin was shot. Neilson shot him. It was an accident, but he's hurt bad. He was trying to get Gabe. Oh my God. I think he's going to die, Annie. There was so much blood."

Neither of us said anything for a few seconds. We were trying to take in everything that had just happened. Then, Annie reached out and put her hand on me, she locked eyes with me, and she said, "Take a deep breath. It's going to be okay."

I struggled but took a deep breath. Suddenly I felt calmer. She was manipulating my energy. She was absorbing my panic attack. Oh my gosh, how was she doing that? I didn't really care. I felt so calm.

Then, all hell broke loose. There was a loud bang, the windshield shattered, and something zipped between us. Annie threw herself over the top of me, shoving me down. I heard whooshing sounds above us. Annie was cursing fluently.

"Goddamnit. Son of a bitch. Motherfucker."

"What the hell is happening?"

"Someone is shooting at us. We have to get out of here, or we're toast."

She threw the car back into gear and started driving without lifting up to look. She didn't want to get shot. We'd barely started moving when there was a loud thud. We'd hit a car as we tried to pull back onto the road.

"Shit," Annie yelled. She swung her door open and jumped out, leveling her gun at an old lady. The lady threw her hands up in the air, looking terrified.

"Ma'am! Get down!"

Clearly, she was not who shot at us. Annie swung around as I went to get out of the car.

"Stay down! Don't get out of the car."

The car was smoking. I thought I'd better get out anyway. I jumped out and noticed there was a black SUV across the road. Annie ran around to my side of the car as I saw the window was rolling down just barely. A gun poked out the window and Annie threw herself on top of me. There was a loud cracking noise, and Annie was bleeding from her shoulder.

Oh, my God. She was shot. What the hell was I going to do? She was on top of me, and my ribs were hurting bad.

I craned at an angle and reached for my cellphone, but it wasn't in my pocket. It must have been in the car.

Annie raised up a little bit. "I'm okay. We have to get out of here right now." We heard a car door shut. I looked up just in time to see the flash of large boot approaching before everything went black.

Chapter 30

As I came to, there was a real nasty metallic smell around me in the pitch blackness. Blood. It had to be. I always knew the scent of blood. It's unmistakable in its coppery scent and the way it makes my stomach churn. I had no idea where I was, but I suddenly felt the pain in my rib cage and head. It was so bad I could barely breathe. And then there was the smell, so I wasn't sure I wanted to breathe. I was in a tiny, cramped space. I couldn't move my hands or my legs very far without hitting solid walls of some sort.

    I reached out and felt around me. Slick and slimy wetness on some sort of fabric. It felt like I was moving. Oh my god, I was in the trunk of a car. Who's car was it? The booted man? Gabe's? Then, I remembered Annie. Oh my God, she was shot. What if she was dead? My emotions went haywire.

I continued trying to feel around the space I was confined in. I couldn't find anything but what felt like an old wrench. Whose blood was this? Was it mine? My head was throbbing like it was going to explode.

I focused hard on any noises that I could hear. I wanted to see if I could tell where I was at or where I was going. I felt the car stop. Then it started again. This time there was a lot of bumping and jostling. It seemed like we might be on a dirt road now. It didn't feel like pavement. This went on for quite a while.

As I listened, I realized I could hear noise in the car. It sounded like someone was talking. I could only hear one side, so I was assuming it was on the phone. I strained my ears, praying to catch a few words. I couldn't.

Then, I opened up my senses. Maybe I could hear through my energy. And just like that, I knew this man was Gabe. Unfortunately, I also knew that the booted man wasn't anyone I knew. As I focused, I could hear Gabe's thoughts. I guess in the time I was out, they transferred me to Gabe's car. Oh my God, this blood could be the blood of his decapitated victims.

That thought hit me like a sack of potatoes. I was horrified. I was petrified. I was utterly disgusted. I tried to calm my energy, so I could focus on listening to Gabe's thoughts.

"I have her. I'm going back to your house now. We can take care of her there."

My mind raced. Take care of who? Probably me. Oh crap. That didn't sound good all. That meant he wanted to kill me, but why?

"Make sure you follow the plan. Everything needs to happen fast. Draw him in, and then we end it. I want this wrapped up by tonight. No chances of anything going wrong."

Wait, draw who in? Apparently, I wasn't the only one they wanted to take care of. Misery loves company.

There was silence for a few moments. Then, "No. I said stick to the plan or your next. We aren't screwing this up. Get the trash bags ready. Prep the bathroom. I will be there soon."

Oh, my God. This was too much. I was going to die. He was going to kill me and cut me into pieces. I hurled. It was dripping all over me, but I couldn't even bother caring. I was really going to die like this—not a shred of dignity.

I felt the car hit regular roads again. He must have been taking the back way where he was going to avoid traffic and possible suspicion. I guess driving around with a person and trunk full of blood might make a person scared to get stopped by a cop. That and he was on the run.

After a few more minutes, I felt the car stop. I was waiting to feel it start again. Then I heard the car door open and close. This was it. It would all be over soon. At least I'd probably die quickly. When the trunk opened, I realized it was dark outside. We appeared to be in some sort of alley. How long had I been out? He looked down at me.

He looked so average, not like what you would imagine a killer to look like. He didn't have red eyes or a cold face. It was almost boyish, the type of person you'd smile at on the street. He stared at me with a look of disgust on his face. Apparently, he can handle blood, but vomit was too much for him. Go figure.

"Oh, look who's awake now," he said.

He grabbed me by the hair and yanked me out. I opened my mouth to scream, but he shoved something in it. He dragged me by the hair towards a gate, through a backyard, and into a door that appeared to be the back of someone's house. Great, I had no idea where I was at all.

When we were inside the house, he drug me into the kitchen. He shoved me into a chair. I tried to get up, but he shoved me back down and started wrapping my wrists and ankles with zip ties. He bound them so tight I couldn't move them at all. He then wrapped a rope around my body, so I was attached to the big, hard, wooden chair I was in. He was humming calmly.

    Instead of fear, I was beginning to feel numb. This was it. Everything would be over soon, at least I hoped. This wasn't forever. I could survive anything for a short while. This was nothing but a temporary predicament. As he left the room, I started to pray. It seemed like I should probably make my peace with God since I'd be dead soon enough.

Chapter 31

It seemed like I was alone in that kitchen forever. It was a rather bland little room with very little personality. It had outdated appliances and a refrigerator void of any pictures. The sink was full of dirty dishes swarming with flies, and the cabinets had seen better days. The only part that was warm and inviting was the cute little curtain over the kitchen window. You know the type that hangs at the top and is just for decoration? Well, I couldn't remember the name for those, but this one had ladybugs on it and flowers.

I could hear distant noises in the other part of the house, but I didn't care to try and listen. I just wanted it all to end so I wouldn't have to wait anymore. Waiting to die is like the worst curse. Knowing it's coming, but having to ponder over it. I'd always said that I wanted to die fast or in my sleep, so this was my own personal form of Hell.

You see, I'm not the type of person who has spent a lot of time thinking about my death. We are all going to die sometime. We are dying from the day we're born. That's what aging is. What I have spent a lot of time thinking about is the death of people I care about. I always hope they die peacefully in their sleep, or at the very least, fast and no time to suffer. The thing that was bothering me now was that I didn't know if I'd suffer long or if I'd die fast.

Eventually, Gabe reentered the room. He brought Anthony with him. Anthony looked pale and tired. He also looked terrified. He ordered Anthony to help him lift me. They each grabbed hold of the chair and took a side. This poor man! He was abducted, and he was being forced to help hurt other people. At least he was alive. There was that.

They carried the chair out of the kitchen and down a hallway. They placed me in the bathroom. The time was here. Finally, it was over. No more waiting. Then, they left and shut the door to the bathroom.

What the hell? Couldn't they just kill me and get it over with. This was worse torture than anything else they could do to me. The bathroom was also a sad little place. The shower curtain had a dolphin on it, but it looked like the cheap kind you get for a couple bucks at the dollar store. The rug on the floor was dirty and could have used a good fluffing. The vanity was filled with medicine and hygiene products. The mirror had a large crack in it. Basically, this bathroom was as uninviting as you could get...well the blood I was dripping wasn't really helping it. It could probably be a little worse.

I was suddenly filled with sadness. This little place was so tired and boring. I was going to die here, and this was the last thing I'd see. I wished I was on the beach or maybe out in the sun, not in this little windowless hell.

I hoped my mom was able to keep Ozzie happy. He adored her, but he was my baby. He slept with me and everything. He was going to be so sad.

Now I was getting angry. I wasn't going to die here all complacent. I had a dog waiting on me. My mother would be devastated. I needed to help rescue my friends if they weren't already dead. If they were, I needed to avenge their deaths and put this bastard away for life. I'd promised Ozzie I'd pick him up from the vet. I had to get out of here. I just had to.

Then, the bathroom door swung open. I threw my weight at it as fast as I could. I wasn't going down without one hell of a fight. My chair toppled over and smacked into the door, slamming it shut. I felt my ribs give another sudden spark of pain. Gabe was on the other side of the door cussing like a sailor.

"Listen here, you little bitch," he said. "when I get this goddamn door open, I'm going to fucking kill you."

I pressed my weight into the door, doing my best to jam it where he couldn't get it open. I had no idea what to do next, but this was a start. I could hear all kinds of commotion outside the door. Then, all of a sudden, someone started kicking the door. With each thunk, I felt more pain in my side. My arm was pressed up against the bottom of the door, but I couldn't move it.

I felt a sharp stabbing pain in my forearm, and I realized Gabe had plunged a knife under the door. "Gotcha, you bitch," he yelled. My arm poured drippy, goopy blood onto my already bloody body. It was a deep cut, but nowhere that convinced me I was knocking on death's door. I stood a chance. I just needed a plan.

He continued to yell through the door. "When I kill you, I'm going to make it slow and painful. I'm going to make you wish you'd never met me, you little whore. You're gonna fucking pay."

Did he think I didn't already wish I'd never met him? What a fucking idiot.

Chapter 32

There were several minutes of Gabe fluently cursing before anything really happened. He shoved his hand under the door, which while it wasn't very effective at getting me out, did prove to provide quite a lot of information for me. When his hand connected with my bare skin, I got the most vivid flash I've ever had.

I was looking through the eyes of someone else. It was like we were one person. I could hear their thoughts. I could feel their surroundings. We were on the trail, not far from the lodge. I recognized the area. The air, clearly early morning with grass full of dew, felt moist around us. Our breathing was labored as we continued trekking along.

I felt our body getting more tired by the minute. We needed to rest, but we kept walking. There was nowhere near to take a seat, so we didn't have much choice. The person was thinking. They were thinking about getting healthier, and how they had to shove, or they'd never lose the weight. They didn't want to die of heart problems. They wanted to get their life together. They wanted to get married and maybe have a couple of kids. It was too late.

As we continued to walk, we realized that we needed to find a bathroom. We remembered that there was a lodge not far from here, so we headed in that direction. As we walked, we noted how alive we felt. We noted the air on our skin and the feeling of the rough terrain under our feet.

As we approached the lodge, we realized how urgently we needed to use the bathroom. Our stomach was hurting bad. Damn breakfast burrito. We hurried and swung the door open. As we started through the door, we recognized the old landscaper on the floor a little way away. Oh, my God! We wondered if he was dead.

As we approached, we saw the other man in the room. He was holding a huge machete. It was covered in blood. We noticed that the man on the floor was missing one arm, and that's when we realized what we had just stumbled upon. We were interrupting a murder.

We panicked as we tried to turn around and run back out the door, but the other man was far too fast. He ran after and knocked us on the head. As we went down hard, we saw the machete coming down at us. There was so much pain. It wouldn't end. The man drug us back into the lodge.

He placed us on the floor next to the landscaper whose eyes were wide and unblinking. He was dead. There was blood coming out of us, and all over the floor we were laying on. We soiled ourself. We thought we'd surely die soon, but with each blow from the machete, we just felt more pain. The man was smiling down at us.

Then, I was back. Without a doubt in my mind, I knew I'd just witnessed Wilson's brother's murder. It all made sense now. He was killed for interrupting the murder of the landscaper. He wasn't killed as a target. He was an afterthought. He was an inconvenience. He was nothing but a loose end.

No wonder he was so angry. He had chosen life. He'd decided to work hard and do better, and this asshole had chosen to kill him. I felt the anguish he had felt, and I wretched on the floor. The pain was fading the further away from the vision I got, yet in some ways, it was still screaming in my ear. I could hear his fear as he spluttered as he was mutilated. I couldn't think about that, though.

I could still hear yelling outside the door, but clearly, some time had passed. I didn't know how much, but I did know that I had more evidence now than the entire police department. I knew why at least one man was murdered.

I had to figure out how to tell someone. I didn't know if I could project my energy far enough, especially not knowing where I was, but I had to try. Maybe I could reach Neilson or Calvin. I centered my energy and focused as hard as I could. I couldn't find Calvin anywhere. I hoped he wasn't dead. I could distantly feel Neilson, but I was having a hard time connecting to him.

After several attempts, I connected. "I need help!" I said.

"We are looking everywhere for you. Where are you?"

"I don't know. There was an alley, and then a kitchen. Now I'm barricaded in the bathroom. Is Annie okay? Is Calvin?"

"Annie will be just fine. Calvin's just out of surgery. They think he's going to be okay. We need to find you. I'm going to get my best trackers tracking your energy. Hang in there. Stay in that fucking bathroom."

"I'm trying. I know what happened. I got a vision. Wilson's brother was killed for interrupting the murder of the landscaper. He was not targeted. He was just a mistake, an unwanted interruption."

"Shit. Okay, that's why the connection hasn't been popping up. He wasn't targeted. We will find you. We will save you, Reba. Are you hurt?"

"Yes. I've been stabbed. I think my ribs are broken. I think I have a concussion, but I'm alive."

"We will find you. Just hang in there."

And then there was nothing. But there was hope. The people I cared about were alive. If nothing else, I had that to die with.

Chapter 33

After what felt like a very long time, I managed to barely shift my weight. I was going to try something, but I didn't know if it would work. I wanted to use my energy to break the zip ties. In theory, I could focus in on sending energy to my hands, and I might be able to melt them with the heat I produced. So far, I'd managed nothing. The longer I focused my energy though, the more I felt the zip ties getting warm. Slowly they moved from warm to hot. Eventually, they were burning my skin, but I didn't stop. I kept going. Finally, I popped my hands free. I had several very bad burns, but my arms were free. I had weapons again.

Then, I started on the rope. I pulled it free with relative ease. The feet wouldn't be that easy, though. I didn't seem to be able to push my energy into my feet. I wondered if it was because the energy push I was doing before had momentum, starting in my feet, shifting up my chakras and body. I couldn't reverse it for some reason.

If I shifted off of the door and they realized it, they would bust in. Then, I'd be dead. I contemplated this. If I could shift the chair to block the door, I stood a chance. Just how to accomplish it?

I'd have to risk them noticing. I could not walk with my feet zip tied. In as swift a movement as I could manage, I pulled myself from the floor and shoved the chair under the knob. It made a huge whooshing noise which caused a lot of commotion again. "What the hell are you doing in there?"

I needed to make quick work of these ankle ties. I crunched over, causing a lot of pain, and grabbed the zip ties. I focused the energy into my hands and felt the ties grow hot then I yanked them off. I had more burns on my hands, but it wasn't something I couldn't handle. There was a lot of banging on the door, and I knew I wouldn't get long before they got the door open. I couldn't just wait around for someone to find me, though. I needed to take action.

My arm was still bleeding rapidly, so I dug in the cabinet for some gauze or something. There was none, so I used some medical tape to hold a wash rag on my arm. I started looking for anything that could be used as a weapon. I found a razor and a pair of scissors, but otherwise, this bathroom was useless. It was a random shit that would only help if I wanted a facial.

With a loud bang, the door swung open. I didn't even have a chance to use my weak little arsenal of items I'd found. I was grabbed hard enough that the pain in my side was worse than I'd ever felt before. Gabe drug me out into the hallway and back to the kitchen. I clawed at him with my fingernails, but he seemed to barely notice. He shoved me on the ground. Then, he handed the gun to Alice, my pregnant client.

"Don't let her fucking move. You hear me?" he spit out. She nodded as he left the room. The pain in my side was almost too much.

"Are you okay?" I asked Alice.

She said nothing, just nodded. I felt like I was going to pass out. Every inch of my body started burning. My head felt like it was on fire, and my vision started to blur.

Then, I was gone again. I was at the police department. I was at Wilson's desk. I was Wilson. His phone rang. As he answered it, I heard Gabe on the other end of the phone. "If you ever want to see your brother alive again, you better get your ass to 1942 Fern Street. Don't tell anyone. Don't tell your boss. If you do, your brother will be dead before you get here."

"Who the fuck is this?"

"It's your worst fucking nightmare if you don't get to 1942 Fern Street. You have half an hour or he's dead." The phone went silent.

Then Wilson was looking around the half-empty room. His anxiety was ramping up. He felt a lot of pressure to do the right thing, but he was scared. A cop whose name I didn't know, said, "Who was that?"

"I don't know. A prank call, I think."

"What did they say?"

"I don't know. Didn't make much sense. Don't worry about it."

He slowly got up and moved toward the door. Someone asked him where he was headed, and he said he needed some air. He was plotting in his head. He knew he had to go. He had the address, and he got in his personal car. He was headed straight to rescue his brother. He owed him that much. He'd never really had his back. They started using drugs together, but he never got caught. He'd let his brother get fried for it, and he never came clean about him being the first one to use.

Then, I was back. I was lying flat on the dingy floor. Alice was looking at me with curious eyes, but she said nothing. Somehow, I knew that this time, it was a vision that was happening this minute. Was 1942 Fern Street the address of the house I was at or a different one? Maybe I should try to get back in touch with Neilson. Either way, he needed to go save Wilson. There was no way that he was going to rescue his brother since I have been talking to his ghost. He was going to die.

Chapter 34

I didn't move for a while, I just stayed still. I was trying to connect with Neilson, and it wasn't working. After a little while, I sat up, and Alice pointed the gun at me again. She must have been terrified. She wouldn't even talk to me. The stress couldn't be good on the baby. I felt awful that I'd gotten her into this mess. I was going to do my best to save her. I owed her that much.

I finally managed to tune in to Neilson's energy. He was frantic.

"Neilson, I have an address for you. I'm not sure if it's here or not, but you need to get there because otherwise, Wilson's dead. He thinks he's going to rescue his brother."

"What's the address?"

"1942 Fern Street."

"I'll send people straight that way. Are you still in the bathroom?"

"No, I'm in the kitchen. He has Alice holding me at gunpoint. She must be terrified. She won't even talk."

"We are on our way. My trackers can't seem to connect with your energy. They said sometimes strong energy can shield itself. I can't find your energy either. You have to find mine. Don't disconnect your energy. Okay?"

"Yeah. I get it," I said. I was feeling woozy. I'd lost a lot of blood. My heart was racing. I felt all clammy, and my left shoulder was throbbing. I was in so much pain I couldn't move.

I'm not sure how long I sat there before I heard a car pull up outside. Oh God. If this was Wilson, it was going to be bad. Gabe came back in the room. He had another gun in his hand.

"Get up."

"I can't," I said.

"Get up off the floor, or I'll shoot you."

"I can't. Help me up."

He grabbed me and yanked me to my feet. The room swum around me. I heard the front door. Then, Wilson was shoved into the room by Anthony. Anthony immediately left the room again. Where was he going? Why wasn't he being forced to stay put? Gabe looked at Wilson and smiled.

"Where's my brother?" he demanded. He didn't even look at me.

"You'll be with him soon enough," Gabe said. Then he shot him between the eyes. Wilson's body crashed to the ground. Alice started crying. Neilson was cursing in my head. I couldn't believe it. Wilson was lying at my feet, and blood was going everywhere. He was gone. No one could save him, but at least it had been quick. He hadn't suffered. He'd died immediately.

Gabe turned to me. I was leaning on the counter, barely able to stand. "Do you know why I killed him?" he asked.

"No. Unless it's because you're a fucking psychopath," I snapped at him.

I felt Neilson recoil. Apparently, he didn't approve of me losing my temper when I had a gun pointed at me by a man who just murdered someone in front of me. I saw this going one of two ways. I'd piss him off enough he'd kill me fast, or I'd distract him long enough for help to get here.

"You think you're really tough, don't you? I wanted him dead because he'd have come looking for his brother. Then, I'd of got caught. I'm tying up loose ends. I don't want anyone to have evidence on me. Well, we'll see how tough you feel when I cut off your hands."

"Why are you waiting around? Just do it. You're all talk and no action." I was trying to get him mad. Mad people can't plan things out properly. Emotions get in the way.

Neilson yelled at me, "Shut the fuck up. What are you doing, Parker? Are you trying to get him to kill you? We are still five minutes out."

I ignored him. Gabe lunged and grabbed me around the throat. I was furious. I was terrified. All my energy lit up and shot out of me. He yanked his hands back. Then, he crumpled to the floor. He was alive. He was awake, but he was shaking. I went to step past him, and Anthony came into the room. His eyes rested briefly on the dead body on the floor, and then he looked up at me.

Gabe said, "Grab her. She's getting away."

I turned to Alice and said, "Come on. I'm going to get you guys out of here. Hurry. Help is on the way."

She didn't move. Neither did Anthony. Then, Anthony reached to grab me. I shot energy at him. What the hell was he doing? Didn't he want to escape? He also crumpled to the floor. I turned to Alice.

"Come on. Hurry!" I reached for her, and she backed away. Okay, I'd done what I could. I had to go before Gabe recovered. I'd never shocked someone on purpose, so I didn't know how long he would be affected. I staggered towards the door, and I felt a sharp pain in my right shoulder at the same time as I heard a loud crack.

She'd shot me. Well, flippin' flapjack. This situation was getting crazier and crazier. They were in on this plot. She wasn't abducted. She was in hiding. Anthony and Alice were bad guys. How did I miss it?

Neilson had clearly missed that too. He was freaking out. He was cussing and yelling in my head, but I didn't have time to talk to him. I had to get out of this house. I staggered through the door and out onto the lawn.

Chapter 35

It was dark, and I was utterly disoriented. I was bleeding profusely, but I staggered on. I couldn't stop moving. I had to move if I wanted to survive. There were footsteps behind me. I turned around and saw Gabe staggering after me. He was brandishing a huge gun which he fired once. It missed me, though just barely. I tried to keep walking as quickly as I could, but I was getting really dizzy. The pain in my side had reached a fever pitch, and I was about to dissolve into nothing. Darkness was filling the edge of my vision. Clenching anxiety was crippling my intestines.

Bang. Another shot whizzed past me. I picked up my pace. I'd made it a few more steps when another shot rang out. This one grazed my arm. My feet faltered slightly as I stepped in a hole, and I hit the ground hard. This was it. I was done for. He was going to win after all.

Then, I heard the sirens. The blissful screech of sirens was for once welcome. I saw the red and blue lights out of the edge of my vision. I stayed down, praying they were fast enough to get him before he got me. There were squealing tires and yelling. I heard shot after shot ring out over the next ten or fifteen seconds. Then, I raised up just barely. Gabe was on the ground a few feet away from me. He was face down.

It was over. He was dead. I had survived. I HAD SURVIVED!

Then, there were more shots. I pressed myself back down. Anthony was shooting at the police cars. I heard running feet, and then Neilson was on top of me. He was pressing me down to the ground.

"Stay down. Don't try and move," Neilson yelled over all the noise and commotion that was going on.

"I can't move. You're on top of me!" I groaned out.

He didn't respond. Apparently, he didn't want me to complain at him while he was saving my life. To be honest, I guess that's fair. When the shots ceased, I heard the cops rushing around. He rolled off of me, and he pulled me to my feet. They were cuffing Anthony near the front of the house.

They were yelling at Alice. They were telling her to come out of the house with her hands raised. She exited the front door and raised her hands. They rushed at her and cuffed her. I was still in shock that they had been in on the whole thing. I couldn't believe it. I'd thought they were drug into this mess by me, but they must have drug me into the mess. I still couldn't make it all line up in my head.

Everything was getting too fuzzy. My brain couldn't take in much more. The pain in my arm, my shoulder, my head, and my side had hit a point that I couldn't breathe normally. An ambulance pulled up, and Neilson rushed them over to me where I was leaning against a tree. I was starting to fade in and out. I fell down. They lifted me back up and loaded me onto a stretcher, and then there was nothing.

***

When I came to, I was definitely in the hospital. I could see a bland blue curtain hanging as a partition between me and someone else's little room. The fluorescent lights glared down at me, making me blink rapidly. Then, I heard a gasp. I turned my head and saw my mom and Annie, setting by my bed. They stood up and came to my side. Annie smoothed my hair back out of my face.

"Hey," I said.

"Oh, honey!" My mom threw her arms around me. I gasped, and she yanked back. "Oh no! I'm sorry. I hurt you."

"What happened?"

"You're at the hospital. Gabe's dead. It's all over, but you have to have surgery. They are taking you back in a couple minutes. They think you may have ruptured your spleen. You also have to get that bullet out of your shoulder. You're in pretty bad shape, girl. We gotta get you taken care of. They did you in pretty bad," Annie said.

I tried to raise up, but pain shot through so many spots on my body. Annie gently pressed me back down. "Don't move. You need to stay still. They didn't think you'd come to before they got you back. They only reluctantly let us in to see you."

"Are you okay?" I asked her.

"Oh yeah. I'm fine. I self-heal," she whispered.

"You what?" I asked. My brain was foggy. I couldn't imagine what she meant by self-heal. Don't we all self-heal?

"I'll explain later," she said while grinning at me. "I'm okay, though."

I felt my eyes getting heavier by the second. I heard someone enter my little room, but I couldn't keep my eyes open. I drifted away to the sound of my mom saying, "I love you. See you when you get done. I'll be here waiting."

Chapter 36

I could hear voices around me. Through my closed eyes, I could see the glare of bright lights. Someone was fiddling with something on my arm, but I couldn't tell what. I tried to lift my heavy eyelids, but it was like they were glued shut. I heard a female voice say, "I think she's trying to come to. Poor dear is really messed up. Stab wounds, gunshot wounds, broken ribs, a huge gash on the head, and they had to go and remove her spleen since it was punctured from a rib. She's gonna be here for a little while."

God, I didn't sound like I was in too good of shape. I managed to blink a few times. The pain in my stomach was severe. I tried to set up, and a female voice said, "No, no, dear. Stay still. Don't try and move just yet."

I stopped fighting to move, but I finally managed to open my eyes. I looked at the room around me. I must have been in a post-op room. It wasn't the post-op I was used to. Was I not in Stillwater anymore?

"Where am I?" I croaked out. My throat was so dry.

"You're in Oklahoma City at OU Medical Center. You've just had major surgery, Sweetie. Just try and rest," said a very grandmotherly looking nurse who was smoothing my hair out of my face. She had kind eyes and laugh lines. She looked like the type of woman who would hand you a cookie and a glass of tea if you entered her home.

"Can I have some water?" I asked.

"Yes, yes. Here you go." She put a cup and straw up to my mouth. I sipped, but she took the cup away quite quickly. "We don't want you to get sick. That's enough for now."

I laid there, feeling extremely drowsy. I wanted to stay awake, but I was having a lot of trouble. The room had swirling colors around the edges, and I could hear all the nurses talking. Their voices echoed as if they were down a long tunnel. I could no longer make out what they were saying. I drifted in and out of consciousness.

Eventually, I felt my bed moving. I opened my eyes, and I saw them rolling me down a long hallway with lots of doors. The walls were alabaster colored. I'm sure the tiles were equally bland. It was a typical hospital. They rolled me into an elevator. There were two nurses there. I asked, "Where are we going?"

"Shhhh, Honey. We are taking you to a room. Don't worry. We have you. Just keep resting," said the grandmotherly nurse. I liked her. She was kind. I felt safe enough to doze back off into sleep.

***

I opened my eyes. I was looking up at a plain white ceiling. I was hurting, but not as bad as I had been last time I was awake. My room had light streaming in, so my eyes burned from the stark contrast. I felt a hand take mine.

I turned my head sideways. Calvin was standing there.

"Hey there," he said.

"Oh my God. You're alive," I croaked out.

"Yep. Much more so than you. You gave us all quite the scare."

I tried to sit up, but pain seared out along my abdomen. I gasped.

"Yeah, you probably shouldn't do that. Do you need me to get a nurse?"

"No, they will just give me more drugs to make me sleep. I want to know what all happened."

"It's probably good you don't want a nurse. I smuggled Ozzie in to see you. He's been so distraught."

I turned and saw that a big duffle bag was wiggling on the chair near my bed. It was unzipped. Ozzie poked his head out.

"Mom! Mom! Mom! You're alive. They didn't kill me at the vet. I've missed you so much. I forgive you for leaving me there. Mom! Mom! Mom!" Ozzie said in rapid fire.

I snickered a little, but it hurt like hell. Calvin scooped Ozzie up and brought him to the edge of the bed. "Now, be quiet. They'll kick us out if they catch me."

I lifted my hand and stroked Ozzie. He licked all over my fingers. Calvin eased him back into the bag. He just poked his head out.

"I don't even know what day it is."

"It's been about twenty-four hours since you had surgery. You've been in and out, but you couldn't stay awake. They had you on massive amounts of drugs."

"How are you up walking around?" I asked.

"Oh, it wasn't as bad as it looked. As soon as they got the bullet out, I was good to go. I self-heal, apparently."

"What the hell does that mean? I think I remember Annie telling me that she does too."

He laughed. "Yeah, it's weird. Some people have what is called accelerated healing. It doesn't always work, but when it does, we can heal something that would take weeks in a matter of minutes or hours. I had no idea about it until the doctors couldn't find the hole for the bullet a few minutes after my surgery. It was pretty hard to explain. I checked myself out before they started treating me like a freaking science experiment."

"That's insane," I said. "I wish I could self-healed."

"Yeah, it's pretty useful. I wish I could heal you," he said in earnest.

"What about Anthony and Alice?"

"Oh yeah. That's a mess. They will go down for a really long time."

"How were they involved? I couldn't make sense of it. I thought they were being held against their will, but they weren't. They must have been in on it."

"They were in on it. Alice copped to the information almost immediately. She wants a plea deal. Apparently, Gabe approached her after the photo shoot. He said if she cooperated and helped get at you, that he would pay her a ton of money. I guess she and Anthony have been pretty broke, so she called him and asked his opinion. He was totally thrilled to make a few thousand bucks."

"Oh my gosh. That's crazy. She was never taken?"

"Nope. They put her in hiding. They wanted to use her to get you, and then they planned on taking the money and relocating."

"When you say they, who do you mean?"

"Gabe and Anthony, of course."

"No, there was another man too. He is the one that shot at Annie and I. He was a huge guy."

"No, there wasn't another man," Calvin said unsurely.

"Oh, yes, there was. When I came to, I was in a car trunk. That other vehicle was an SUV. It didn't have a trunk."

Calvin looked at me, reluctantly. "Well, we haven't found any evidence that there is another man, but I will tell Neilson. He has been damn well worried about you. I need to tell him you're awake."

"Did Annie not mention the man?"

"She has a nasty concussion. She's suffering from some memory loss. They didn't catch it at first, but then her head was hurting worse and worse, so they got her checked out. A severe concussion. She can barely remember something someone said to her five minutes ago, so I bet she can't remember."

"Damnit!" I growled.

"Hey there, calm down. You're safe. We'll catch them if there is someone else. Don't worry about it right now. You need to rest."

A nurse came in at that moment. "GET THAT DOG OUT OF HERE!" she bellowed at Calvin. He leaned down and gave me a quick smooch on the forehead. He turned and scooped up Ozzie who was growling like crazy.

"I'll be back in a bit," he said as he quickly shuffled from the room.

The nurse wandered around my room, wiping everything down like Ozzie had contaminated it. She fretted over me until I asked her if she knew if I had my cell phone. She dug through a bag of things and handed it to me. She left the room. I dialed my mom.

"Mom?"

"Oh, honey, I've about ten minutes from the hospital now. How are you feeling?"

"I'm okay. Tired, but okay."

"I've been so worried about you." She sounded weepy. Uh-oh. I'd put a lot of stress on her the last few days.

"Don't worry, Mom. I'm tough. Calvin just left with Ozzie."

"Did he get caught?"

"Yep, but I loved on him first."

"Calvin or Ozzie?" my mom asked with laughter.

"Very funny. I meant Ozzie," I said, laughing gently. I gasped.

"Oh, don't laugh. That can't feel good."

"It doesn't, but I'm alive, so that's enough for now."

Chapter 37

It felt like they kept me in the hospital forever. By the end of the first week, I was by far stir crazy, but they wouldn't let me go home. They told me I had to stay for several more days. They wanted me to recover under observation. I started whining incessantly. I'm NOT good at being a patient. I've spent plenty of time in the patient chair, but I've never been good at it. It felt like you weren't supposed to be good at it if you know what I mean.

The hospital food was like cardboard. Daytime tv was boring, but I did have lots of visitors. By day four, Annie was doing better and coming to visit me. My mom spent a lot of every other day with me. Calvin came every single evening. Neilson came every couple of days. I was overwhelmed with the love that everyone was showing me.

As much as I wanted to dislike Neilson, he was turning into quite the fatherly figure in my life. Since I hadn't talked to my dad in I don't know how long, it was weird to have Neilson fussing over me. Every time he came, he snuck me in french fries and a milkshake. We'd sit there and talk about anything and everything from the weather to my photography business.

On day ten, Neilson must have finally thought I was feeling better enough to talk about the case. Every single time I'd brought it up before, he's said I didn't need to waste my energy thinking about it. Day ten was different.

Neilson had been there a little while when he said, "So Calvin and I have been looking for the other man you said was there. We can't find anything. Do you think when you get out of here, you could work with Courtney to get a sketch?"

"I'll try. I'm not sure if I got a good enough look, but maybe I will be able to give at least a general description."

"Anything would help. If there was another guy, he might be long gone, but we want to nail that bastard if he's not. We'll put everyone on high alert if we can get a description. We'll draw him out by being discrete, making him think we don't know about him."

"Okay. Can she come here? I'll try now," I said eagerly.

He laughed. "Why don't we wait until you are out of the hospital? It can wait a few more days."

Neilson met my mom the day I was being released. It was day fourteen, and I was getting restless. I'd ate my awful food, and chugged liquid to prove I was okay. I'd walked all around the floor and was really shoving to impress my doctor. I missed my bed and my dog. Also, I missed my cameras.

When Neilson showed up, I was dressed and waiting on discharge papers. I introduced him to my mom, and my mom got all flustered. She said, "Rosie here has told me so much about you. I'm glad you've had her back. I'm so grateful you saved her life."

She was flushing. What in the world? It was like a schoolgirl with a crush. Neilson was smiling and putting on quite the chivalrous show. Ewww.

She told him that she was going to go grab a cup of coffee, and she asked him to join her. He obliged, and they left me alone to wait for my paperwork. I wasn't sure how I felt about them walking off together like that. I definitely wanted her to be happy, but I wasn't sure if I wanted her to be happy with Neilson. It was kind of weird. I really couldn't remember her ever dating. She and my dad split when I was just five or six years old.

No matter how I felt, they clearly hit it off quite well. They were like smitten teenagers by the time they returned. I'd had to call my mom twice to get her to answer the phone. That never happened. There was a rather sing-song tone to her voice when she answered. "Hu-low!"

"I'm ready. I'm just waiting for you to come up and grab the stuff. Then, you need to pull the car around."

"Okie dokie, Sweetie. I'll be right up," she said.

When they'd got there, Neilson stayed with me while she went to get the car. He said, "Your mom is just wonderful. You're lucky to have her."

I muttered about knowing because I did, but I didn't want to talk to him about her. As soon as I was all loaded up and home, I called Calvin.

"You wanna know something?" I said.

"Sure."

"I think Neilson and my mom have a crush on each other. They even exchanged numbers."

"No way," said Calvin. "I've never seen him date. I know he's been married before, but I think she died a real long time ago."

"Yeah. Well, they were like little lovesick birds calling out to one another. It was crazy."

"Does your mom date?"

"I literally never remember her dating."

"Who knows, maybe it will be good for them both," he said hopefully.

"Huh," I said.

"I'll come over as soon as I'm off work. If you need me, text me!"

He got off the phone, and I puttered around the house with Ozzie right at my feet. My mom had tried to keep him for me, but I wouldn't have it. I had missed him like crazy.

Over the last couple of weeks, my mom and I had talked about my abilities. She said that she had a lot of ability before she had a car wreck a few years back. She sustained a head injury, and she'd never quite recovered all of her abilities. She didn't really mind though. She said having them had always been more of a curse than a blessing for her, which I did totally understand.

I'd asked her why she never talked to me about them, and she said she was afraid that I would tell people about mine. She knew what it was like to have people treat you like you were insane. Apparently, when she was growing up, her parents had briefly had her committed because she was hearing voices. In that day and age, you were a nut job if you were different.

While I understood her reasoning, I had been a little annoyed that she'd let me struggle without telling me I wasn't nuts. I guess it goes to show that sometimes when we try to save someone, we end up causing a little damage ourselves.

After wandering around my house, I decided to take Ozzie out for a short walk. I didn't have much energy yet, so I didn't make it very far before we turned around and came back. When I got back to my house, there was a very concerned looking Annie beating on my door.

"Oh my gosh," she said. "Where the hell were you at?"

I laughed. "I was just walking Ozzie. What's up?"

"You aren't supposed to be wandering around by yourself yet. You aren't back on your feet."

"Oh, come on. I just walked down the block a little ways. It's no big deal, really."

"Excuse me for being worried about you almost dying," she said sternly. It reminded me of how Kate used to treat me.

"Okay, okay!" I said, raising my hands in defeat. "Let's go inside."

Once we were inside, I told her all about the conversation I'd had with my mom, about Neilson and my mom, and about how Calvin was coming over later. She was as shocked as I felt about my mom and Neilson. She told me all about his past marriage. Apparently, he'd been married for ten years when his wife died of a sudden brain aneurysm. She said that she didn't know his wife that well because she'd always kept to herself. They didn't have kids because she had been infertile. Annie thought that she was always a bit reclusive because that had broken her heart, but she had died when Annie was just ten years old, so she didn't really know for sure. It sure gave me a lot to ponder. Maybe I was going to have to come around to the idea of him and my mom.

Chapter 38

That night Calvin came over. We watched a movie together. Things were quite tense between us. There was a definite spark, but of course, with me healing up, he'd been very hands off. Ozzie cuddled between us on the couch, and it was just a nice, quiet evening—at first.

Neilson showed up as the closing credits were playing on our cheesy rom-com. He knocked on the door, and Calvin got up and let him in. He could tell he might have interrupted something, and he looked around awkwardly. Well, he hadn't really interrupted anything, but I still kind of stared at him mean like. Then, I invited him for a glass of wine. After all, this man had been checking on me day and night the last two weeks.

He accepted, and Calvin poured him one. He sat down in the recliner, and Calvin took his seat back beside me. Ozzie ran over, and much to everyone's surprise, jumped up in Neilson's lap. We all froze.

Then slowly, Neilson stroked Ozzie's head. "Hey there little guy," he said.

"Hey ya'self! Thanks for saving my mama. Grandma told me you helped take real good care of her."

Neilson laughed, "Of course, little buddy." He stroked his head. Then, he turned and looked at me.

"First off, you were right. I did shoot Calvin, so I owe you an apology."

"No, you don't. It was an accident. I thought you were going to try and kill him. You clearly didn't."

He shrugged.

"All the same. I have a question for you," he said.

"Mm'kay?"

"Do you want to properly learn to use your ability? I mean like to undergo training from people that know about it? You are the strongest psychic I've ever met. You need training. You're a danger to yourself without proper training."

I thought about it for a minute. "Well, I'd been thinking about asking you for more information. You see, for some reason, my ability has been getting stronger and stronger lately."

"Unfortunately, the more you tap into your ability, the stronger it gets for a while. You accidentally unleashed your ability."

"Well, crap-a-carport. That's not good."

Calvin snickered beside me. He'd told me he loved my creative little not quite swear words. You see, I try really hard not swear, but sometimes I mess up.

Neilson watched me. "Yes," I said. "I want to know more."

He looked at Calvin. "What about you?"

"Me?" he said.

"Yeah, you. It's about time you learn how to use your abilities. You could use them to help a lot of people."

"Oh," Calvin said pensively. "I guess that's true. Okay."

"Well, then, I will let people know."

"That sounds awfully cryptic," I replied.

"Well, there is an entire organization of people, of psychics, that exists. Some of them have day jobs. Some solely train other psychics. Some are in law enforcement. Some contract with law enforcement. The common theme though: they all learned to use their ability, and when they can, they help other people with their gifts."

"Do those 'people' have a name?" I asked.

"The organization is called UPC, Unprecedented Psychic Cooperative. If asked, they just leave out the word psychic."

"Oh, it sounds official."

"It is," he said.

Calvin was silent. He clearly was intrigued, but unsure if he was interested. I think his ability scared him. He frowned at me, and I closed down.

"We'll need to learn more if you want us on board," said Calvin.

"Of course," said Neilson. "Let me get in contact with a few people, and then we'll go from there. In the meantime, you can look them up. There isn't much info online though. You can also ask Annie. She had official training when she turned eighteen. She actively consults on cases across the country. She also helps train others, as do I."

"Okay, so who are these people you need to let know?" I asked.

"Oh, the organization leaders, Marvin and Misty. If I can't reach them, I'll contact their son, Mason. Sometimes Marvin and Misty are a little flighty when they are working a case. They like to specialize in cases with paranormal elements, but they will take other cases like cold cases when needed."

"Are they cops?" Calvin asked.

"Yes, and no. They consult, but they have ties to the FBI, the CIA, and all kinds of people. I don't even know who all they are affiliated with."

"That sounds serious," said Calvin.

"To be honest, it is, but the more you know, the better off you are. I think it's worth it, or I would have never told you."

"You better hope we agree," I said. I was feeling somewhat reluctant all of a sudden. I wanted to know more. I wanted to know how to control my ability, but I also didn't know if I was prepared to be part of this grander plan or picture.

"I feel sure you will agree that it's more than worth any nerves you have about it. No matter what happens, UPC folks always have each other's back. With their help, you'd have been found before you were taken, most likely. They were trying to help me find you."

"Oh, so those are the people that you had trying to track me?"

"Yes, and they were quite curious at the strength of your energy. They will be elated to meet you. Oh, and they pay if you do any consulting. They make sure you are always paid a solid wage. If you aren't, they sweep in and handle the situation."

"That's good," I said.

"I guess," thought Calvin. We'd started talking to one another in our heads. We had learned we could wall up our thoughts, and no one else could hear us. Neilson suspected as much, but we hadn't confirmed to him.

Neilson said, "Look, I will call you tomorrow or the next day. Rest up. I will be in touch with them, and we'll go from there.

Chapter 39

I didn't hear from Neilson for three days. I was getting annoyed by the time he showed up. Then, he arrived at my door at 7 AM. I was wearing a big t-shirt and booty shorts. I hadn't even got up when I heard the loud knocking on my door. I'd staggered through my house to peek through the peephole when I found Neilson, a younger black man, an older white man, and an older black woman standing on my steps. The three oldest looked calm and carefree, chatting jovially, but the younger man who appeared to be near my age looked nervous.

I opened the door a little reluctantly.

I said, "Hello?"

"Did we wake you?" asked the woman.

"No," I lied while trying to stifle a yawn.

She laughed. "Oh dear. We must have. My apologies. We just got in and were eager to meet you."

"Sorry," I yawned. "But I'm not sure I know who you are."

Neilson jumped in. "Sorry, Reba. This is Marvin, Misty, and their son Mason. I mentioned them to you the other night."

"Oh yeah," I said awkwardly. Now I realized what a mess I looked before these people I barely knew. My clothes were a rumpled mess.

"Oh, never mind that. You were put through hell recently," said Marvin.

I flinched.

Misty said, "Marvin, get out of the poor girl's head. You're going to scare her off."

Mason extended his hand. "Sorry for the early wake-up call. They never listen to me. I did tell them it was much too early to call on someone unannounced."

He looked to be a little more at ease now. "Oh, no worries. Come in, come in." I said. I was suddenly wide awake. As we went inside, I grabbed Ozzie up, but he seemed utterly non-bothered by our guests.

I excused myself to my bedroom to get dressed. As I pulled on a t-shirt and some sweatpants, I scrutinized myself in the mirror. It would just have to do. I still couldn't stand the pain of wearing real pants on my stomach.

I left the bedroom, and I leashed Ozzie and took him for a brief bathroom break in the yard. When I returned, Neilson had retrieved the orange juice and poured glasses as I'd asked him too.

I put on a pot of coffee and turned to be seated at my table. They were all looking at me rather expectantly.

"Sorry," I said. "I don't wake up very fast."

Misty smiled warmly. "Neither do I. I'm a bear for the first couple of hours. Take your time, Dear."

She wasn't what I expected. She had gorgeous hair to her shoulders. Her eyes were alive and sparkly. I imagined a severe-looking woman with a tight bun, not the type of woman one felt compelled to speak to on the street.

Marvin wasn't what I imagined either. He was tall with relatively average features, but his smile was warm. I guess I hadn't spent much time thinking about Mason, but he wasn't what I would have expected as the prodigy of two strong psychics. He had boyish features, at least his face. He was broader shouldered than his dad but had the same warm smile and kind eyes his parents had. They looked absolutely ordinary, not like leaders of a secret organization.

After a few minutes of relative silence, I finally asked, "So what next? Do you guys tell me things, or do I ask questions?"

"Oh, we have plenty to tell you," said Misty. "But you have to sign a contract first."

I felt myself blanch. "Uh... I don't know."

Mason laughed. "She's kidding. Mom, I told you to stop saying that. It freaks people out."

I laughed nervously. Well, at least there wasn't a contract. As the coffee finished brewing behind us on the counter, I stood to get it. Misty shushed me away with a wave of her hand, which I noticed was covered in bright gemstone rings. "No worries, no worries. Let me, Dear. Do these mugs work? I know this one is your favorite, so I will give it to you."

I flinched again. These people were kind of weird. "Yeah, those are fine," I said.

After we all had a big mug of coffee, Misty and Marvin jumped into a long explanation about what they did. Most of the information I'd either found on a deep dive online or Annie had already told me. I wasn't surprised to hear that both Marvin and Misty got their start in the CIA. That's where they learned to use their abilities. The CIA had trained them. They didn't like being part of the CIA with all the rules and backstabbing, so they made their own organization and started building a network. Some thirty years later, here they were in my kitchen, meeting another newbie. This was just another normal day on the job for them.

They explained that I could do consulting work, but I could also just accept the training and never take a single case. It was entirely up to me. They made this organization to help people, including people with abilities that needed guidance. This made me feel a lot better than I did when I thought I had to work with people, and when I'd thought I would have to put my life on the line. I was considering the consulting, but I needed more time to adjust.

All of the anxiety I'd been feeling recently felt like it was draining out of me. I felt hope rearing up in me for the first time since I was drug into this mess. I'd been having trouble centering myself recently, and I was able to pull my energy up each chakra and breathe almost normally again.

Maybe, just maybe, this was all going to be a good thing. I'd almost wrapped my head around everything, when Misty smile brightly at me and said, "So whatcha think? When do you want to start training, Dear? We have plenty of locations."

About Jenna B. Neece

Jenna B. Neece is a multi-genre author from Oklahoma, a proud dog mom/human aunt, and fighter of many chronic illnesses. Jenna has two creative writing degrees from Oklahoma State University. She taught college for five years. She is author of RAISE A GLASS TO MY BODY. She spends her time writing, reading, gaming, watching tv and movies, and can be found on social media.

Follow Jenna on Social Media:
FACEBOOK: @JENNABNEECEAUTHOR
INSTAGRAM: @JENNABNEECE
TICTOK: @JENNABNEECEAUTHOR
TWITTER: @JENNABNEECE
WORDPRESS: www.jennabneecewrites.wordpress.com

Made in the USA
Middletown, DE
04 December 2022

15969292R00170